Secrets
of
Willow Lane

Secrets

of

Willow Lane

J. L. Anderson

ISBN: 978-1-946195-53-1

Library of Congress Control Number:2019919163

23 22 21 20 19   5 4 3 2 1

Cover and Interior Design: FuzionPress

Published by FuzionPress

1250 East 115th Street, Burnsville, MN 55337

To my husband, Wade.

He knows why.

Chapter 1

The frigid air swept across her face. Her eyelids fluttered as she came to in a daze. Her head ached. Her ears pounded. *Where am I?* She felt the carpet beneath her cheek, and slowly, the fibers came into focus. Her eyes followed the fibers one after the other. Warm. Soft. They blended together forming a sea of white as her gaze wandered farther and farther down the hallway. She knew this hallway.

Her head felt like dead weight as she struggled to lift it. She pushed herself up onto her elbows. Her head bobbed. Her body teetered. Mangled wire spectacles dangled precariously off her right ear, and as she turned her head, they fell silently to the floor. She gazed across the hallway. She blinked repeatedly in an effort to clear her vision. Without the much-needed help of her glasses, she could just barely make out the figure lying motionless on the floor. But it was there. *Oh Dear Lord, what on earth happened?*

She tried to rise, but the ground whirled beneath her forcing her to lower her head back into the sticky pool of blood that had accumulated on the carpet. She closed her eyes in an effort to regain her equilibrium, then rolled onto her back and waited for the spinning to stop. A drop of blood trickled down the side of her face, caught in the creases time had left behind. She felt herself blacking out again and battled the overwhelming urge to succumb to the sleepiness. *No!* She resisted. *Not now, Dear Jesus, not yet.*

She took a deep breath. She reached into her sweater pocket and wrestled out her cell phone, thankful, for the very first time, that Gib made her carry it. She held the phone close to her face and pushed the emergency button. She listened intently, but could only hear the rushing inside her own head.

"Help," she said. It came out as a whisper. *Was anyone there? Did they hear?*

"Help," she uttered once more. Then the hand cradling the phone fell to the floor. As she lost consciousness, something soft brushed lightly across her cheek.

◆ ◆ ◆

Isaac arrived as quickly as he could. He wanted to view the crime scene before too many others had passed through. That initial, undisturbed atmosphere allowed him to get the best insights about a case. And Isaac Scott had a well-known and highly respected track record for having great instincts. Most of the detectives would tell you it was a gift. However, there were times Isaac felt it was more of a curse.

Isaac had a lot of experience under his belt. And although he knew his experience helped, he also knew it couldn't replace the nagging, subconscious, intuition cops referred to as "hunches."

Isaac always began each investigation with a clean slate, never allowing a past investigation to color the next. While one case may show similarities to other cases, they were rarely the same. Each case exposed a new twist, an unexpected wrinkle. Over his years on the force he learned that pat answers didn't exist and easy solutions were rare. People's lives were complicated and multifaceted. What initially appeared to be true was frequently just whitewash. Isaac had an innate ability to breach past the facades and pretenses people used for protection.

Today, unfortunately, another investigation delayed Isaac and he found the avenue already crowded with police vehicles. The news reporters had quickly closed in and a civilian crowd was beginning to form outside the split-level Tudor. The curious bystanders huddled together whispering and speculating despite the inclement February weather.

Isaac pulled in as close as possible amidst the orderly disruption. He ran his hand over his face and took a moment to steady himself for this next tragedy he was about to witness. *Would the violence ever stop? What was it, he wondered for the billionth time, that he loved so much about this job?* The answer came easy. He loved catching the culprits, no doubt about it.

He scanned the customary montage gathered outside. A few officers, who stamped their feet and cupped their gloved hands over their mouths to keep warm, guarded the cordoned perimeter. While the officers repeatedly declined the reporters' persistent interrogations, the press did not relent. With little to no concrete information, they narrated the scene like sports commentators at a boxing match eagerly anticipating the knockout punch. Camera crews hovered, ever ready to catch the scoop on tape. Isaac shook his head. Nothing escaped their scrutiny. Granted, at times the press could be helpful in solving a crime, but at this particular moment, they looked like vultures waiting to feed. They thrived on stories like this. The more heinous, the better. In their line of work, if good news was no news, then without bad news, they'd all be out of a job. Predators without prey.

Isaac surveyed the onlookers, the usual bunch. Titillated neighbors, gossiping and guessing, reminiscing and reflecting. Isaac imagined he'd glean any pertinent information from his colleagues' interviews and reports. Those same neighbors, generally the most familiar with the neighborhood comings and goings, could be a wealth of information and often the sources of the best leads, many times without even realizing it.

Just down the street Isaac noticed a woman who stood away from the crowd. While most bystanders stood as close to the barriers as allowed, she stayed well back from the group behind a stand of mailboxes. Isaac paused with interest. The crime scene door banged open, attracting both their attentions. Uniformed officers quickly cleared a path, moving the throng back from the road. The paramedics carried an occupied gurney to the back of the ambulance while the reporters gave the play-by-play. He glanced at the woman by the mailbox. Even from a distance he could see the color drain from her cheeks. *What could she tell him?* he wondered. Slush splattered Isaac's windshield as the ambulance pulled out and sped past him, sirens blaring.

Isaac turned off the engine and hoisted his six-foot frame out of the car. Frozen bits of icy rain pelted his side as he maneuvered through the crowd. He held up his hand to protect his face, passed through the police tape, and carefully, tactically, made his way to the house. Isaac's shoes sank into the half-melted snow, slipping occasionally on the sheet of ice concealed beneath. He shuffled along like a kid learning to skate, first one foot then the other, doing whatever was necessary to keep from ending up on his rear end.

With relief, Isaac grasped the railing and stepped up under the covered entry. He did his best to brush the moisture from his coat and thoroughly wipe his feet on the already sodden welcome mat.

The door swung open. "Isaac." Vick smirked. "I've been waiting for you." The amused expression on his face revealed he must have been watching Isaac's inelegant arrival.

Isaac noticed Vick was dressed to the T, as usual. Not a single strand of hair out of place. Not a wrinkle in his clothing. Vick's meticulous nature was not only a big hit with the ladies, it also could be a plus in their line of work. However, while Isaac respected his cohort's perfectionism, Vick's constant preening did tend to get on his nerves.

Vick leaned against the railing as Isaac stepped over the threshold. "Glad you could make it."

"Yeah, my pleasure," Isaac responded sarcastically. "Lovely weather we're having," he said as he pulled the door shut.

"Isn't it though? I heard the airport closed down several runways and delayed flights right and left. Something about difficulties with de-icing."

"Imagine that. And they say nothing exciting ever happens in Minnesota."

"Well, whoever 'they' are, they're wrong. This house had more than enough excitement earlier today."

"So I gathered." Isaac sighed. "Let's get to it. What do we have here?"

"One female with a gunshot wound to her head, D.O.A. She's in the bedroom. She's believed to be the homeowner." Vick checked his notes. "One Mrs. Crystal Rutherford Holt. And we have a second female with a nasty wound to the top of her head."

While Vick spoke, Isaac removed his gloves and coat and placed them on the clear plastic draped over the entryway railing. Due to the weather, almost everything inside had been covered with plastic in an effort to avoid corrupting the crime scene.

"She's on her way to Methodist Hospital," Vick said. "Paramedics found her on the hallway floor."

Isaac stepped out of his water-stained loafers. "Who made the call?"

"Female #2."

Vick jerked his head toward the main hallway. "Come down here, but stay to the edge. There are shoe prints down the middle." Vick pointed down the hall. "Take a look."

Isaac immediately noticed the dark red stain on the cream-colored hallway carpet in front of him. Vick moved in behind him next to the wall. From what Isaac could see, the victim had lost a good deal of blood. "How serious was the injury?"

Vick leaned over Isaac's shoulder. "Paramedics said she'll make it. But from the looks of it, I'd say she'll have one hell of a headache."

"What do you know about her?"

Vick flipped open his notepad. "I found a purse by the back entry. The driver's license inside is issued to Edna Louise Rupp of St. Louis Park. Seventy-two years old. I found a coat on the rack downstairs that I believe belongs to her. Some winter boots by the coatrack too. Also probably hers." He flipped his notebook closed. "We don't know what her relationship is to the deceased."

Isaac nodded. He looked left into the bedroom, and his eyes fell on Female #1. Her body lay spread eagle on the floor, as if she had purposely fallen back in that position like kids do to make snow angels. The fingers on her right hand were loosely entwined in the gun. Part of that side of her head was missing. Isaac inhaled sharply at the sight and the stench filled his nostrils. There was no other smell like it. His stomach churned uncomfortably, and he had to look away.

"Oh, man." No matter how many he'd seen before, it never got any easier. Isaac took out a handkerchief and covered his mouth.

Vick slid past Isaac and crossed to the other side of the door frame. "Such a pity. She must have been a real looker."

Isaac flashed Vick a look. Sometimes Vick's preoccupation with appearances came out at the most inappropriate times. "Tell me you didn't just say that," Isaac groaned through the cloth.

"What? What did I say?"

Isaac shook his head.

"Well, she was," Vick declared. "Look at her."

And Isaac did. The robe draped loosely around her, still tied at the waist. She had nothing else on. Her skin was smooth and tanned. She had a dancer's long, firm legs. Her hair, colored like corn silk, encircled her head on the floor. Lying there lifeless, she reminded Isaac of a Barbie doll and was probably one of the few women in the world who could have lived up to that ideal. The sight deeply saddened him. It was indeed a pity, Isaac agreed. Beauty or not.

Vick smoothed his hair with the heel of his hand just like James Dean. "Must have broken some hearts in her time."

Isaac lowered the hanky and stuffed it back in his pocket. He glanced up at Vick. Vick himself had had his heart broken several times by beautiful women. Beautiful women who clearly had nothing more to offer than their beauty. The thought of this made Isaac all the more grateful for his own lovely wife, Claudia. Her timeless beauty shone from the inside out, unlike the fleeting, superficial good looks of the purely physical kind. Claudia possessed substance and character. A woman who, in Isaac's eyes, grew more beautiful every day. He looked back at Crystal Holt. *Had this woman also been more than just another pretty face?* Isaac wondered. Over the next few weeks, he would find out. He would get to know her intimately, postmortem, through the eyes of others.

Isaac noticed the ring finger on her left hand. "Didn't you say her name was '*Mrs.* Holt'?"

"Yup," Vick confirmed.

"I don't see a wedding ring."

"They're probably separated," Vick said. "The poor schmuck."

Vick was probably right. These days it was more the norm than the exception. It certainly had been in Vick's case anyway. "Then am I correct in assuming we're now looking for Mr. Holt?" Isaac asked.

"'Course. Suspect Number One, right?"

Isaac raised his brows. "We'll see." Isaac never liked to jump to conclusions, but Mr. Holt was, without question, one of the first he'd want to talk to. "Any sign of an intruder, a struggle?"

"Door was wide open, but not forced. One broken mug in the sink. Everything is just the way we found it."

Good. Soon he'd get a chance to make his own assessments with as little disruption as possible. "So, what's your initial take?"

"Well, since she has the gun in her hand, it would appear Mrs. Holt committed suicide."

"Then, how would you explain Mrs. Rupp's injury?"

"That is a good question, isn't it? The broken mug would indicate that someone was mad."

Or someone just dropped it, Isaac thought to himself. "Keep going."

"Sure. Looks to me like Mrs. Holt and Mrs. Rupp had an argument in the kitchen. Mrs. Holt hit Mrs. Rupp over the head, then went into the bedroom and shot herself."

Stranger things have happened, Isaac conceded. "Do we know what caused Mrs. Rupp's head injury?"

"Oh yeah, forgot to show you that. We're pretty sure it's that big iron frying pan over there." Vick gestured toward the kitchen doorway, again with his characteristic head jerk.

Isaac stepped across the hall and leaned around the corner of the kitchen doorway, careful not to touch anything. He saw the noticeably out-of-place object laying on the floor partially hidden by the dinette table. It was one of those heavy 'name brand' types with the wooden handles that weighed a ton. The kind Claudia liked to use. Isaac had always been amazed at how his gourmet wife, a petite woman, could so competently handle one. In the wrong hands, however, it was definitely substantial enough to become a lethal weapon.

"That could certainly do it," Isaac agreed. He rubbed his forehead and scrunched up his nose. "So, you think Mrs. Holt hit Mrs. Rupp on the head with the skillet, flung it on the floor, walked into the bedroom, and shot herself with a gun?"

Vick shrugged.

Isaac scratched his head. "Doesn't make sense."

"Hey, does it ever make sense?"

That would certainly make a neat package. No loose ends left dangling. No murderer to find. Isaac tried unsuccessfully to visualize that chain of events. "Then why was the door open?" he asked as it opened below and a blast of cold air tunneled down the hallway.

"Hey, shut the door!" Vick hollered. He pointed at Isaac. "That's what we're all depending on you to figure out."

"They're coming in for the body," a voice called out. "You guys done up there?"

"You got photos of everything?" Isaac asked Vick.

"Yup."

"I need ten minutes alone," Isaac told them.

♦ ♦ ♦

"Marta!" Patty exclaimed as she tromped through the snow and onto the sidewalk. "I didn't expect to see you here."

Marta's stomach tightened. This was definitely the last thing she wanted. "Matt's sick today," she explained.

"Oh no!" Patty's words dripped with insincerity. "What's wrong?"

"Ear infection."

"Oh, the poor thing. I'll bring him some of my famous chicken soup—guaranteed to cure anything!"

Marta eyed her suspiciously. Marta knew better. Sure, Patty would bring the soup—she'd use any excuse to dig for fresh gossip—but Patty couldn't care less about Matt's ear infection. Marta wrung her hands, purposely avoiding eye contact. "Thanks, Patty. How thoughtful of you," she said, then returned her attention to the scene across the street.

"I wonder what's going on over there," Patty said. "I just got home and saw them take Crystal away in the first ambulance. Well," she corrected, "I *assumed* it was Crystal—and then another one pulled up! Now, who on earth could that one be for?"

Marta shifted uneasily on her feet. A bead of sweat ran down her back making her shiver. The frozen rain continued to drip from the sky, coating the mailboxes in front of her with a thin, shiny layer of ice. She grasped the end of the stand to steady herself.

"Everyone's in a tizzy wondering, and the police won't tell us a thing."

The way Patty said 'everyone' made Marta want to gag.

"In fact, they're being downright rude—and we're just concerned neighbors!"

Marta nodded. Sure, more like insatiable busybodies. She squeezed her already tense fists harder, her knuckles turning white inside her gloves.

Suddenly, Patty's incessantly open mouth snapped shut. Her mittened hands covered her cheeks. "Oh, I'm so sorry! I'll bet you're incredibly distraught since you and Crystal are such good friends and all."

Marta wanted to punch her. Patty never had been a good actress. Marta clenched her teeth.

"Well, you just never mind all that," Patty said, dismissing the scene with a wave of her hand. "I'm sure it's nothing. Crystal probably just had a fall and broke something."

Marta stared at her in disbelief. "Sure." She wasn't going there. Not with Patty—not with anyone—for that matter.

"I'm sure of it," Patty said, then exhibited that condescending 'mommy dearest' smile she did so well.

Marta snarled inwardly. *Why won't she just leave me alone?* She kicked a hole in the snow with the toe of her boot. She had enough on her mind without having to listen to Patty's merciless blather.

"I'm just so glad that Crystal has had you two to depend on since their break-up. It's so sad to see that happen. You know your husband has been so good to her," she gushed. "He is just a gem!"

Marta tugged at her jacket collar, as if it were choking her. *Oh God, make her go away.*

"What a nice thing to do—taking her to all Matt's hockey games. I'll just bet it was your idea, though, wasn't it, Marta?" Patty smiled that sick, sweet smile again.

This time Marta couldn't help herself and returned the smile with venom. But as usual, Patty didn't notice and continued. "You two gals are so close! Well, I'll tell *you*, Crystal really seems to enjoy the sport—all that hugging and cheering with every goal!" She glanced sideways at Marta.

Marta stared straight ahead. It was incredible how Patty could get under your skin. Like a bloodsucking parasite, she drained the life right out of you. It took everything Marta had to ignore her insinuations.

"I can tell she's very proud of your boy. I'm just surprised she never had any children of her own. But then, she might lose that fabulous figure of hers."

Marta rolled her eyes. *The green-eyed monster had reared its ugly head.*

"What a beauty!" Patty proclaimed. "The rest of us moms show up in our jeans and sweatshirts—well, just like you and I do, Marta—*you* know," she said, casting Marta in with the rest of the lot. "But Crystal always looks like she stepped right out of the pages of *Vogue*."

Try as she might to conceal it, Patty's jealously came through loud and clear. Marta's stomach turned. Everyone was jealous of Crystal.

"Oh, I hope that whatever happened in there doesn't affect her looks," Patty lied unconvincingly. "What a pity that would be. You know, she's the envy of *all* the ladies."

Suddenly, the door to Crystal's home burst open, finally silencing Patty. Both women watched as the men carried the body bag to the ambulance. Marta's knees went weak.

"Oh, no! It looks bad." Patty crossed her arms over her chest and narrowed her eyes. "Do you think Crystal finally killed that horrible husband of hers?"

◆ ◆ ◆

Isaac peered out the window and watched the crowd as the paramedics loaded the deceased into the ambulance. He noticed the woman by the mailbox was still there, but she was no longer alone. A second woman had joined her. As the ambulance backed out of the driveway, the first woman abruptly turned away and trudged unsteadily east through the snowbank along the curb. The second stared after her, mouth agape, then threw up her hands and set out to join the larger crowd. Isaac focused in as the first woman traversed the street and started up the walkway toward the house at the end of the cul-de-sac.

Chapter 2

Although necessary, Isaac always found it creepy going through a victim's belongings. Their most personal, intimate items were handled and scrutinized. It felt intrusive and unsettling, particularly in this case. So far, they had found nothing to indicate illegal behavior or even disreputable tendencies. No stash of drugs, no cache of weapons, no threatening letters, no lewd photos, and none of the things that somehow made it feel that this intrusion of privacy was warranted and would lead to some understandable reason or cause for the loss of life. Isaac sighed. He turned away from the window, pulled out his memo pad and reviewed his notes to make sure that he had captured all his previous observations.

The Holts' bedroom, where Crystal was found and now only a chalk outline remained, was in complete disarray. Several dresser drawers were open, their contents spilling over and onto the floor below. Jewelry strewn helter-skelter cluttered the dresser top.

The master bathroom, in contrast, was well organized. The vanity drawers contained neatly arranged trays of Crystal's cosmetics and personal items. The medicine cabinet was filled with the standard stuff and more well-ordered than most. Definitely more well-ordered than his own, Isaac had to admit. Claudia always said you could tell a lot about a person by inspecting their bathroom. Isaac agreed.

The room down the hallway held a desk and chair, but no other furnishings. The desk drawers held the standard items: pens, pencils, paper, notepads and a stapler. None of them appeared to get much use.

Isaac closed his notepad and let his eyes move slowly around the living room. It was decorated in the colorless ends of the spectrum with some vibrant splashes of red here and there. A black leather sofa covered one wall and a couple of white chairs sat in front of the bay window. The carefully placed adornments meant the room had been recently cleaned, or possibly, never used. Isaac ran his finger across the chrome coffee table's clear surface leaving a clean line in the thin layer of dust. Never used, he decided.

The door opened in the entryway half a flight below and Isaac listened to Vick's grousing as he stepped through. "This weather sucks," he announced to no one in particular. "I almost killed myself coming up those steps."

"A little slick?" Isaac asked.

Vick smoothed his hair and straightened his scarf. "A little!" he scoffed. "It's a skating rink out there."

Isaac laughed. "Well, keep your coat on. We need to start interviewing the neighbors."

Vick held up his pointer finger and took a breath. "I knew you were going to say that. And not to worry," Vick said as he adjusted his leather bomber jacket looking like he just stepped out of the movie *Top Gun*. "It's already begun."

"Good," Isaac approved. "Oh! But Vick," he called. "Let them know I'll take care of the house at the end of the cul-de-sac."

Vick raised his brows. "Why?"

"Just a hunch."

Mystified, Vick nodded at him slowly. His forehead creased, his eyes narrowed. *Isaac, ever the clairvoyant.*

"Oh, and Vick, get this crowd dispersed. The show's over."

"Yes, sir!" Vick saluted. "But just so you know, Oh Magnificent One, I have a hot date, and need to get going soon."

Isaac regarded him with amusement. "Don't worry, you'll have time to fix your hair."

"Yeah?" Vick placed a drenched foot out in front of him. "But what about these alligator Oxfords? They cost a fortune!"

Isaac shook his head. "Get outta here. Maybe next time you'll invest in some good, practical boots."

Vick spied Isaac's soggy loafers. "Like you?"

"You're not the only one with a hot date."

Vick sneered. He pulled up his collar and resignedly headed back into the cold.

Isaac felt the rush of frigid air slip in as Vick slipped out mumbling something about moving to California.

Isaac walked slowly across the living room toward the dining area. He stood and viewed the unadorned space. Other than a large glass-top table in the center of the room and a large crystal chandelier mounted directly above, the room was completely empty. Without any substantial furnishings to absorb the noise, Isaac's footsteps echoed as he moved across the wooden floor. *Did anyone ever actually eat here?* He wondered. Isaac laughed as he thought of what his three children would think of having a see-through table like this. They wouldn't be able to hide food in napkins or sneak treats to the dog under there.

An unsealed Federal Express envelope sat on the clear surface. Isaac picked it up with gloved hands. Inside he found several cards with paint colors and countertop samples and a hand written note that said: *Take a look at these and get back to me tomorrow—Marta.* Next to the envelope sat a small, gold-colored decorative basket with a red Valentine's Day banner suspended between the sides of the upright handle. Nestled inside was a red velvet jewelry box. Isaac opened it. The indentation for a ring was empty.

He put it back and checked his watch. He hadn't been kidding. He really did have a date. It was almost four o'clock and his dinner reservations were for seven o'clock. Claudia would be unhappy if he were late, but he would be more so. This was their night. Not only Valentine's Day, but also the anniversary of their engagement. He patted his coat pocket. The small box, so similar to the one he just inspected, was still there. Isaac warmed at the prospect of watching Claudia's face as she opened it. He loved surprising her. Being married to a cop was no picnic—the irregular and unpredictable hours, working holidays and weekends, and his frequent preoccupation with cases even when home. She put up with so much. He was so lucky. Not many spouses were as understanding. He'd seen many couples crack under these adverse conditions. He didn't know what he would do without her. She was his sanctuary. She deserved this little token he carried and much, much more. He couldn't wait to place it on her finger and see her eyes sparkle—a sparkle that would outshine the stone itself. The anticipation of that moment moved him along.

He took another look around the kitchen from the doorway. The forensics team had already begun dusting for prints, so he did not enter. A partial pot of coffee sat on the countertop still warming. One coffee cup sat by the sink with lipstick along the edge, and another in pieces inside. Isaac hoped the mugs would provide the investigators with tons of information through prints, saliva, etc. Amazing things could be discovered from such everyday items.

"Hey Joyce," he said to one of the squad. "Could you dust the coffee maker and get it turned off, please?"

"Sure, Isaac," she said. "We should have some pretty good prints for you here."

"Hallelujah! Oh, and Joyce, keep your eyes open for a ring."

"If you're looking for jewelry, there's a ton in the bedroom."

"Right. I should clarify. A ring that's found outside of the bedroom."

"Got it. Will do."

"Thanks. I'm done up here. I'll be just a few minutes downstairs."

"Fine." She stood up and stretched her sore back. "Take your time, we'll be at it for a while yet."

Isaac descended the stairway keeping to the side. At the bottom, he took a right into the family room. The décor mirrored the same monochromatic theme as the upper level, except this time, the effect was much more inviting. Instead of black leather, the sectional was a heavy cream corduroy. Instead of chrome and glass, the tables were of black iron and whitewashed wood. Plump, fringed pillows abounded, and a flat screen TV hung on the wall. But all the cushy furnishings just provided a backdrop for the most prominent adornment of the room, a large oil painting suspended above the fireplace. A portrait of the deceased, Crystal Holt, wearing nothing but a crystal pendant. The necklace dangled just at the dawn of her generous breasts, cradled in the valley in-between. A gold leaf setting attached the sizable stone to the delicate chain around her neck.

In the painting, Crystal was laying in repose on a fluffy, cream, sheepskin rug. The most private parts of her body were strategically hidden without giving the pose an unnatural appearance. Isaac took a moment to consider it and came to the conclusion that, if he ever had a similar painting of Claudia, which he wouldn't mind, he certainly wouldn't put it on display. *Something like that was too private—or should be,* he thought.

The door slammed above. The wind was picking up. "Hey, Isaac," Vick called as he carefully descended the stairs.

"In here," Isaac responded.

Vick turned the corner. "Oh, now I see what's keeping you. Incredible, huh? Could barely pull myself away either." He placed his fists on his hips and gazed admiringly. "Man-oh-man, would I love to take that home!"

Isaac sighed and turned to look out the window.

Vick continued to stare in silence, lost in the landscape of Crystal Holt's perfect body. Then he abruptly whacked his forehead with the heel of his hand. "Oh yeah, I almost forgot what I came in here for." He crossed his muscular arms over his chest. "Isaac, you never cease to amaze me. You just gotta tell me, how did you know?"

Isaac turned toward him. "Know what?"

"About the lady at the end of the block."

"What about her?"

Vick gaped. "Oh, now you're pissing me off." He pointed an accusing finger. "*You* know. That she's Crystal's best friend."

"She is, huh?"

"Come on, Isaac. How'd ya know?"

Isaac shrugged. "I didn't. I noticed her outside."

Vick shook his head, stupefied.

"What's her name?" Isaac asked.

"Marta. Marta Coburn."

"Marta," he repeated. "Well what do you know. Thanks, Vick."

Unbelievable, Vick thought to himself. He gestured toward the stairway with the jerk of his head. "Okay if I go now? Everything's in motion. Reports should be piling in over the next few days."

"Sure, I'm just finishing up."

Vick pointed down the hall. "That's where I found Edna Rupp's belongings."

"Good. Thanks."

"Oh, and the cat's in the laundry room," he said.

"Cat?"

"Yeah, we found it curled up next to Mrs. Rupp. Appeared to be very fond of the old lady. Anyway, it started roaming around, getting into things so I put it in the carrier in there."

"Did you make arrangements for it?"

"'Course. You know what an animal lover I am."

"Oh, right," Isaac challenged, surprised Vick would even touch an animal for fear he'd get fur all over his clothes.

"The vet will be putting it to sleep tonight," Vick goaded with a smile.

Isaac glared at him.

"I'm kidding, Isaac—just kidding."

"Your depth of compassion forever amazes me."

Vick slapped him on the back. "See ya, partner. Wish me luck."

"Which young lady tonight?"

"Chardonnay."

Isaac scowled. With a name like that she had to be half his age. "Good luck," Isaac offered sincerely. In his opinion, Vick would need it. Especially since the poor young woman's parents had been bereft of sanity, at least long enough to name her after a bottle of wine.

Isaac entered the laundry room and found the cat carrier on top of the dryer. Two green eyes peered out at him. "Hiya kitty," he said.

The cat brushed its furry cheek against the metal screen inviting Isaac to pet it. Isaac stuck a finger through and gave the cat a scratch behind its ear. The cat purred and rubbed against the screen. Isaac began to pull his finger away, but a small paw stretched out through the cage pleading for more.

"Oh, you poor thing," Isaac cooed. "Kinda lonely in there, huh?" He opened the door and lifted the cat into his arms. He stroked its head and the cat snuggled against his chest. It was all black with long, fluffy fur that made it appear larger than its weight betrayed it to be.

Isaac saw the litter box to his right, set the cat down and closed the laundry room door. "Need to take care of business?" he asked. "It may be a while until you get another chance." The cat rubbed against his legs, uninterested in taking advantage of relieving himself. Isaac picked him up and placed him in the box. "Come on now, you're going to wish you had," he warned.

The cat immediately jumped out, flinging granules off his back paws, and went back to weaving around Isaac's legs. Isaac laughed and picked him up. "Oh, okay." Isaac relented and rubbed him under the chin. "But, you'll regret it." The cat didn't seem concerned and purred happily in Isaac's arms. "You've had a big day," Isaac said. "Too bad you can't talk. I sure could use your help."

After a few minutes, Isaac returned the cat to its cage. "Sorry, kitty. Gotta go. But I'll make sure we get you taken care of."

As he gathered his coat and gloves and put on his shoes, he saw the forensics team finishing up for the day.

Chapter 3

The doorbell startled Marta and stopped her in her tracks. She had worn a path back and forth in the carpet since returning home an hour earlier. She peered through the front window at the large black man waiting on the stoop. She resisted the urge to pretend she wasn't home and pulled the door open a crack. The blast of cold air felt surprisingly good. "Yes?"

"I'm Detective Isaac Scott." Isaac held out his badge for her review. "May I ask you a few questions?"

Marta's heart pounded. "Here?"

"Here, would be fine," he responded. Then he smiled and added, "But inside would be better."

"Oh, sure. Of course," Marta said, opening the door for him. "Come in, Detective."

Isaac stepped inside. "Please, call me Isaac." He held out his hand.

She returned the handshake. "I'm Marta."

Isaac closed the door behind him and removed his soggy shoes.

"This is about what happened at Crystal's, isn't it." It was a statement, not a question.

Isaac nodded. "Yes."

"I knew you'd come. I've been worried sick. Please sit down." She gestured left toward the living room.

Isaac sat in a chair across from the sofa.

Marta began to sit and then stood upright. "Can I get you a cup of coffee?"

"That would be nice, thank you." Isaac watched her walk unsteadily down the hallway. He could hear the dishes clatter from the kitchen as Marta assembled the tray.

She poured two cups of coffee and set them on saucers. Her hands shook as she placed them on the tray. *Pull yourself together, girl.* She looked over at the corner cabinet. Knowing she shouldn't, she pulled out the whiskey and added a shot into her cup. That would help calm her down, she assured herself, then took a swig from the bottle to steady her nerves.

Isaac perused the room from his seat. *Lovely. Attractively appointed. Warm. Comfortable. The framed photos scattered about on the mantle and bookshelves added a homey feel.* He picked up the picture on the end table to his left. He recognized Marta seated by a campfire with a man he assumed was her husband, and a young boy Isaac guessed was approximately seven or eight years old.

Marta returned with the tray. Her hands trembled as she handed a cup to Isaac.

"Thank you."

"Cream or sugar?"

"No, black is fine. Is this your family?" Isaac pointed to the photo.

"Yes." She sat on the sofa and took a drink from her cup. "My husband, Blake, and son, Matthew."

"Nice looking young man." Isaac returned the frame to its place.

"Thank you." She clasped her hands on her lap and looked at the floor.

Isaac took a sip.

"I—I heard the news reports," she said. "Do you have any idea how this happened, Detective?"

Isaac returned the cup to the saucer. "That's what we're trying to find out," he said.

She looked up at him expectantly.

"I understand you and Crystal Holt were good friends."

She reached for her cup. "College roommates." She took a gulp. "I've known Crystal for a long time."

"I need to find her relatives." Isaac removed his notepad from his jacket. "Can you help me?"

"Yes." She looked toward the ceiling. "Her um …" she hesitated, unsure what to call him. The title just didn't sound right after all that had happened between the two of them. But yet, it was what it was. "Husband. He's in a townhouse in Burnsville. I can get you the address. Her folks are both deceased."

"The husband's name?"

"Garrett. Garrett Holt."

"Are they separated?"

"Yes."

Isaac wrote the name across the top of a page in his notebook. "Could you write the address here for me?"

"Sure." Marta set down her cup and went to the desk in the corner. She jotted down the information from the address book and handed it back to him.

"Thanks."

Marta sat stiffly in her seat. She bit her lip. *Garrett. He would certainly be the one everyone would suspect*, she thought to herself. "Do you think he killed her?" She gestured toward the paper he had tucked into his notebook.

Isaac cocked his head with interest. "Do *you* think he killed her, Mrs. Coburn?"

"He would certainly be the one everyone would suspect," she repeated out loud.

"Was their relationship contentious?"

"No, but …" She looked toward the ceiling. "Well, sort of."

"In what way?"

How was she to answer that question? "Well, honestly, he wasn't a very nice man. They argued a lot. Crystal needed attention. Garrett just wanted her money."

"Her money?"

"Yes. When her parents died, she inherited a *very* substantial sum."

"How about Garrett? What is his financial situation?"

"Fine, I think." She lifted her cup and took another sip. "Crystal got tired of him always bothering her for money, so she set him up with his own account."

Isaac sat back in his chair. "You said they were separated. Do you know if they had drawn up any divorce settlement documents?"

"Oh yes. I know Crystal did. She was always threatening to file, but as far as I know, she hadn't yet." *But then again, it appeared there were many things she didn't know.*

Isaac paused and took another sip of the warm coffee. He noticed that Marta's cup was almost empty. "Other than her difficulties with her husband, did Crystal have any enemies, Mrs. Coburn?"

Marta shook her head. "She didn't have many friends," she said. "But no enemies either." *At least not until this morning,* she didn't add.

Isaac scratched his head. "Do you know an Edna Rupp?"

Marta shifted in her seat and clasped her hands together. "Yes. She's Crystal's cleaning lady. Why do you ask?"

Isaac saw her fingertips turn white. "Mrs. Rupp was at the Holts' house with Crystal this morning."

"Will she be okay?" Marta asked anxiously.

"Mrs. Rupp is under care at Methodist Hospital. I'm sorry. I have no updated information on her condition."

Marta nodded and gulped the last of her coffee.

"How did Crystal get along with Mrs. Rupp?" he asked.

She set her empty cup on the saucer. "They got along fine. Edna is just a wonderful woman. She put up with Crystal's idiosyncrasies. Crystal would say that Edna was a little meddlesome at times, but it was only out of concern for Crystal. Crystal could have appreciated her more, but they never had any problems that I'm aware of. Edna took good care of Crystal—like she would a daughter."

"In what way did Crystal feel she was meddlesome?"

Marta rubbed her temples with her forefingers. "Oh, I don't know. I shouldn't have called it *meddlesome*. She just mothered Crystal. Like telling her she should eat better and not drink so much. Things like that. That she should get rid of Garrett and find herself a nice man, have a family. You know, that kind of thing."

Meddlesome sounded like an accurate description to Isaac—at least that's what they called it when his mother-in-law offered personal advice. "Did they argue?"

"Not really. Edna, bless her heart, would always listen to Crystal's problems. But Crystal would just cut her off if Edna tried to help."

Could it be that Vick was right? Isaac picked up his coffee. "Her problems? Do you think Crystal suffered from depression?"

"Depression? Heavens no." Marta sat back in her chair and rolled her eyes. "But Crystal was always suffering." She used finger quotes around the word suffering.

Stopped in mid-sip, Isaac looked at her over the rim of his cup.

Her fingers covered her mouth. "I'm sorry, I shouldn't have said that. It's just that Crystal was Crystal, you know?"

No, he didn't. But Isaac nodded, urging her on.

"She just couldn't seem to think of anything from any other perspective than her own. It wasn't always bad, you understand, but …" She sighed. "Crystal couldn't tolerate not getting her way."

The back door slammed and Marta jumped at the sound. "Marta! Marta!" Blake called out. "There's police tape all around—" He stopped short as he entered the living room and spotted the two of them.

Marta looked over at her husband. "Blake, this is Detective Scott."

Isaac rose to shake his hand.

What's going on?" Blake asked.

"It's Crystal," Marta answered. "She's dead."

"She's what?" He looked back and forth between the two of them.

Isaac, still standing, gestured toward the couch. "Perhaps you should sit down, Mr. Coburn."

Blake sat next to his wife. "I can't believe it. How did she die?"

"The news reports said she died from a gunshot wound," Marta answered.

"Oh God." Blake cringed. "I—I don't understand. Was there a burglar?"

"We are looking at all possibilities," Isaac said.

Blake rubbed his forehead for several minutes then reached over and stroked his wife's hand. "Thank you for stopping by Detective." Blake stood. "Please keep us informed."

Marta looked up at him from the sofa.

Isaac raised his eyebrows but didn't budge. "I'd like to ask you a few questions, if that's all right."

"Certainly Detective, but can't we do this another day? It's such a terrible shock for us."

Isaac pursed his lips. There wasn't much he could do about it, but at the very least he could try to get a few more questions in on his way out. "Your wife was just telling me she didn't think Mrs. Holt had any enemies, would you concur with that statement?" Isaac looked at Blake and reluctantly removed himself from the chair.

"Enemies? No, Crystal had no enemies. People liked Crystal. Crystal could be quite generous."

Marta looked down into her folded hands. *Yeah, when it suited Crystal's purposes.* It had always been that way with Crystal. But even still, they had been friends. In reality, she had probably been Crystal's only true friend. "You must understand Detective, Crystal and I go way back. I loved her like a sister and I knew her better than probably anyone." Her eyes teared and she looked into her husband's face. "The good and the bad." She leaned over to pick up the coffee tray. "Crystal was fun to talk to—certainly never boring. She had a good sense of humor and was very social. But, the truth is the truth. Crystal did what Crystal wanted for Crystal's own reasons."

Blake nodded in agreement. "Crystal was a unique individual, Detective. Beautiful, kind—yes, a bit self-centered—but never *intentionally* cruel."

Marta watched him as he spoke, listening to his eulogy. *How on earth could this have happened?* It was all so mind-boggling, so confusing, so sad, and so wrong.

Blake began moving toward the door.

"Just one last question," Isaac said as he followed Blake. "Had anything been troubling Crystal lately?"

"No," Marta sputtered. The dishes on the tray rattled. She leaned over and placed the tray back on the table. "Crystal had been happier lately than I've seen her in a while."

"Mr. Coburn?" Isaac slipped into his shoes. "Had you noticed anything?"

"No." Blake turned the doorknob. "Crystal was quite happy. I'm sorry, Detective, it's just too hard to talk about right now." He pulled the door open for Isaac. "Give us a few days."

Marta handed Isaac his coat.

"I'll be in touch."

Chapter 4

Isaac's foot slipped out from under him as he got into the car. He caught himself with the steering wheel and pulled his body inside. The toughest part of a Minnesota winter could be just getting where you needed to go. Yesterday the ground was covered with snow, today the snow began melting with the rise of the thermometer. Over the course of a few short hours, the morning's snow had warmed to rain and, then suddenly, cooled to sleet. Now, as the day wore on and the temperature continued to drop, all that melted snow would turn to ice. Ice was the worst. He started the engine and turned the defroster on full blast. He picked up the radio and called the station.

"Peg, Isaac here. I've got the address of Crystal Holt's husband."

"Want me to send a squad car?"

"No, I'll take care of it."

"How did I know you were going to say that? Is Vick with you?"

"No. He had to go primp for his big date."

"Tsk, tsk. When's he going to stop chasing after those bubbleheaded teenagers and go for a solid, levelheaded woman like me?"

"Ah ha, be careful what you wish for, Peg. Besides, he doesn't deserve you."

"Right as always, Isaac. But still, if he asked real nice, I'd probably give him a chance—and you can tell him I said that. Anyway, need some back up?"

"Nah. I'll be fine."

"Let me know if you change your mind. I'll be here all evening. Seems I'm the only one without a date tonight."

Isaac signed off and picked up his notepad. While the frost cleared from his windshield, he jotted down his observations from the interview with the Coburns.

He put the car into four-wheel drive and drove carefully across the slick roads toward Burnsville. Maintenance trucks worked tirelessly spewing salt to clear the pavement for the evening rush hour, turning the ice into slush.

Isaac pulled alongside the curb in front of a row of single-level townhomes. Each had a short driveway leading to an attached garage that jutted out the front of the building. Isaac turned in and parked close to the overhead door. No reason to walk any further than he had to in this kind of weather. He followed the sidewalk around the outside to a nicely sheltered entry tucked around the back of the garage.

He knocked at the door and looked around for a mat to wipe his feet on. Finding nothing of the sort, he stamped in place to remove the snow from his shoes, and waited for Garrett Holt to answer the door. Nothing. He rang the bell and heard some activity inside. Shortly, a shadow covered the peephole, and the door opened a few inches, the safety chain preventing any further movement.

The man in the doorway was big. Even bigger than Isaac. He was at least six feet, four inches tall—and muscular. His neck alone was the size of most men's thighs. His blond hair was cropped short—practically nonexistent on the sides—with a perfectly flat plateau on the top of his head. His penetrating blue eyes glared at Isaac. Isaac momentarily wondered if he'd made the right decision in coming alone.

"Mr. Garrett Holt?"

"Who wants to know?"

Isaac held out his badge. "Detective Isaac Scott, Mr. Holt. May I come in?"

"No."

"Are you Crystal Holt's husband?"

"Yeah. Why? What's she want?"

"It's a little sensitive."

His eyes narrowed. "Let me guess. You've got the divorce papers."

"No, no divorce papers. Maybe I should come inside, sir. You may want to sit down."

"No. Just tell me here."

Isaac hesitated.

"Oh, I see." Garrett sneered and his square jaw jutted forward. "She doesn't want me coming around anymore, is that it?"

Isaac raised his brows. "Have you been around?"

"Yeah, yeah. I've *been around*." He scowled condescendingly. "But you already know that, don't you? What did she tell you? That I got rough with her? That I threatened her? Jesus, she's so full of shit. She's the one who threatens. She's the one who gets rough. It was just another fight, so what? What else is new?"

Isaac looked him straight in the eye. "Mr. Holt, Crystal is dead."

Silence.

He looked at Isaac skeptically. "Oh, come on. That can't be."

Isaac watched him closely. Was that fear he saw flash across Garrett's face? "Please Mr. Holt, can't we discuss this inside?"

Garrett's brow furrowed and he closed the door.

Isaac stood firm, deliberating if he should knock again or just go, when he heard the safety chain being removed from the inside. The door opened. Isaac stepped inside.

He saw a large room with the kitchen at one end and the living space at the other. Isaac's jaw dropped as he took it all in. Complete chaos. He hadn't seen a mess like this since visiting the Phi Beta Kappa fraternity house on the University of Minnesota campus after one of their society members got plucked from the Mississippi River.

Garrett grabbed a seat cushion off the floor and shoved it into the chair. "You can sit here."

Isaac couldn't help himself. "Cleaning lady on vacation?"

"I, ah, was looking for something." Garrett headed to the refrigerator. "I need a beer. Want one?"

"No, no thank you." Isaac tiptoed through the clutter toward his assigned seat. "Did you find it?"

"What?"

"What you were looking for—did you find it?"

"Oh. No," Garret said into the refrigerator.

"Ah. What was it? Something important?" From the looks of it, it had to be incredibly important. *Important enough to commit murder over?*

"Um. My wallet."

"Ah."

Garrett cracked the beer and dropped onto the couch. He took a long, hard gulp and wiped his mouth with the back of his hand. "That's some news. How'd she die?"

Isaac folded his hands in his lap and leaned forward. He watched Garrett intently as he spoke. "She was shot."

Garrett cringed. "She was shot? Jesus! Where?"

Isaac wasn't sure if he was asking where as in what was her physical location at the time of the shooting, or where as in the placement of the bullet on her body. He decided to answer the former. "At home."

"Shit! Any idea who did it?"

"That's what we're trying to find out."

Garrett scowled. "What do you mean by that?"

"What I mean is that we are collecting evidence and questioning people who knew her to try to determine what happened. We will appreciate your cooperation and any information you can supply. And, being that you are her husband, we will need you to come down and identify the body and help us with the investigation by answering some questions regarding Crystal."

Garrett nodded, gulped down the rest of the beer from the can, and crushed it in his fist. "Okay, when?"

Isaac made a quick assessment. "We'd like you to make the visit to the morgue as soon as possible. I can send a car to pick you up. They can be here within half an hour."

Garrett's eyes widened. "A cop car?" he blurted out. "No, no way." He waved his hands back and forth like a football referee indicating no score. "I'll drive myself."

Isaac eyed the empty beer can. "We offer rides to the bereaved since it may not be the best time to operate a motor vehicle."

Garrett stood, towering over Isaac. "I don't think you heard me. I'll drive myself."

Isaac looked up at him from his seat and didn't budge. Man, he was jumpy. Not distraught, not bereaved, just completely on edge. "Suit yourself. I'll tell them to expect you within the hour."

Isaac watched Garrett visibly decompress.

"Okay," Garrett said and sat back down.

Quite unusual. Clearly the interview should take place at the station and would take a while. Isaac wanted to be thorough. Even more, he wanted to be prepared—more prepared than he was at the moment. "I'll need you to come to the station tomorrow, say 11:00 a.m.?"

"Make it noon."

Isaac nodded, reached into his coat pocket, pulled out a business card, and wrote the morgue's address on the back. He held the card out to Garrett. "The morgue's address is on the back. My office address and phone number are on the front. See you at noon tomorrow."

Garrett took the card and flipped it back and forth in his fingers, then slid it into the front pocket of his flannel shirt as he stood. He took in a long, deep breath. "Unreal," he muttered as he made his way toward the door.

Isaac's thoughts exactly. He stood and followed. "Hope you find it," Isaac commented, noticing the rectangular bulge in Garrett's back right pocket.

"I'll be there."

"No, I mean your wallet. I hope you find it."

"Oh yeah. Thanks."

Isaac stood in the doorway. "Just one more thing. What would you like to do with the cat?"

"Hmpf, I don't want it. Take it to the pound."

♦ ♦ ♦

Isaac returned to his car and picked up the radio. "Peg, it's Isaac. Put a watch on Mr. Garrett Holt."

"Our perpetrator?" she asked.

"Good question."

"Undercover surveillance or can I just send a car?"

"Undercover, please." *Don't want to spook him,* Isaac thought to himself.

"It will be done," Peg confirmed.

"I'll sit down the block until they arrive."

"Well, then I'd better get someone there quick so you can get home to Claudia."

"Thanks, Peg. Appreciate it."

"No problem."

"Hey Peg, you like cats?"

Chapter 5

Marta looked out the kitchen window at nothing in particular. "I didn't know you'd be home tonight," she said. "I thought you had a meeting."

Blake wrapped his arms around her waist. "It's Valentine's Day, I wanted to surprise you."

"Today has been full of surprises."

He laid his head on her shoulder. "Not the happy sort."

"No. Not the happy sort."

"Is Matt awake?"

"He's watching a movie, feeling a bit better."

"Good. Have you told him yet?"

"No. He slept most of the day. He feels bad enough as it is. I think it can wait." *It could wait indefinitely,* she thought but did not add. She didn't feel up to the task. She didn't know if she ever would. She didn't feel up to much of anything just now. It amazed her how days could go by and turn into weeks and then into years and everything remained status quo. And then, in one day, in one hour, in one tiny moment, everything changed. Things you had grown to depend on, count on, to take for granted—even to the point that they became somewhat annoying at times—were suddenly gone. Why? How?

"I need some time alone," she said.

Blake released her and watched her walk down the hall and into the living room. This day had brought quite the turn of events. Just earlier today he had dreamt how special this evening would be. His eyes welled up. "Okay, I'll go check on Matt. Then I'll make us some dinner." Blake climbed the stairs heavyhearted. The very romantic evening he had so carefully and excitedly planned was not going to be.

◆ ◆ ◆

Red watched as the automatic garage door opened. Garret backed his red Jaguar out of the driveway. Red phoned in. "Peg, he's leaving, I'm following."

"Roger that," Peg replied. "So, Red, you got the Valentine's Day shift too?"

"Well, yeah. What else have I got to do?" Red's real name wasn't Red, but it was what everyone called him due to his thick mane of fiery red hair. Even people he didn't know called him Red, it was just the natural thing to do.

He was a good Irish Catholic and was secretly crazy about Peg. "He's heading north on 49th. I'll keep you posted."

"I'll be here," Peg said.

Garrett turned north on Highway 169 and headed for the morgue. Red watched Garrett enter the morgue at 6:00 p.m. and twenty minutes later he was back in his car and pulling out of the lot. He retraced his route heading south on Highway 169, but passed the exit that would take him home. He crossed the river on Highway 41, then headed toward Mystic Lake Casino. *Interesting destination for a man who just lost his wife,* Red thought.

They both pulled into the parking lot. Red found a parking space just one row back from Garrett. He followed Garrett in and watched him make a beeline for a pay phone near the restrooms. Even on a weekday night, the casino had a lot of activity making it easy for Red to follow Garrett closely without risking detection. Red took a seat at the nearest slot machine. He watched Garrett deposit a quarter and dial a number.

"It's Garrett." Red heard him say.

"No, I don't have the money, but I will soon," Garrett said. Red's ears perked up and he tried to move closer.

"No, she wouldn't give it to me, but—" Garrett was cut off mid-sentence.

"But there's more—" he said in a louder voice as if trying to talk over the person on the other end of the line. Garrett rubbed his now glistening forehead.

"No, just listen, LISTEN," he shouted. "She's dead," Garrett said louder than he should have. He looked around to see if anyone was listening. Red pulled the lever on the machine, then "accidentally" dropped his cup of quarters in Garrett's direction.

"Yes, dead," Garrett repeated in a quieter voice. "All of it will be mine. It'll just be a matter of time." He listened to the voice on the other end.

"I don't know how long, but wait, just wait," he pleaded. "I'll get it all to you."

"Tomorrow? But I can't …"

Garrett furrowed his brow and called into the phone "Hello? Hello?" He pulled the receiver away from his ear and looked at it, then slammed it into its holder. He began to pace back and forth, and almost stepped on Red's hand.

"Whoa, watch out! Klutz below!" Red flashed a big, toothy smile. "Dropped all my winnings." He laughed. Red's best undercover work was done right out in the open.

Garrett scowled at him. Red stood up and walked back to his seat at the slot machine. Garrett pulled out another quarter, dropped it into the phone and dialed.

"I need ten grand," Red heard him say.

"So? So?" Garrett blustered. "So what if you already paid me? You're going to keep paying me as long as you want me to keep your little secret. Here's the deal, when I ask for money, you give it to me."

Garrett listened momentarily, his tension obviously building, then continued with his bullying. "Hey, hey! Stop right there," Garrett commanded. "Don't bother me with your problems. Just get it. I'll meet you at the usual time and place tomorrow. And you better be there you little twerp."

◆ ◆ ◆

Marta sat in the dark living room and took another long taste of her martini. She heard footsteps coming through the foyer. Blake stopped under the arch, his eyes scanned the dimness for her. "Kitchen's cleaned. I'm going to head upstairs." He gazed at her silhouette in the darkness. "You doing okay?"

She sighed audibly and looked off in the distance. "Talked to catty Patty today." She took another sip and swirled the liquid around slowly in the glass.

"Oh?"

"She's doing a good job living up to her reputation. God, she's such a busybody."

"I think it's a requirement that every neighborhood have one."

Marta shook her head in disgust. "She knows everything that's going on with everybody. Of course, the one day that something like this happens, she's not home."

"Not home?"

"Nope, gone all day at some fundraising event." She took a deep breath. Crystal's death was not the only shock of the day. "She told me Crystal has been going to Matt's hockey games with you."

"Oh?"

"I didn't know that."

"I didn't think you'd mind."

"You never mentioned it."

He was going to have to be very careful here. "I didn't think it was important. You know Crystal, ever since the separation she's been in need of something to do, something to fill her time."

"Some attention," she corrected.

"Yeah, I suppose so," he agreed. "But Marta, everybody needs attention sometimes." *And over the last few months Crystal had been getting a lot,* he thought to himself. But he couldn't reveal that.

She shifted in her chair. "So how long has this been going on?"

"A few months. She really seemed to enjoy the games."

"I heard."

What had she heard? he wondered.

"Patty said she was cheering and hugging every time the team scored."

He shrugged. "You know Crystal."

Boy did she ever.

"Well," he said. "I'm going to head to bed. Love you, honey."

She raised her glass in response.

He turned, crossed the foyer and headed upstairs.

Marta downed the last gulp of her martini and laid her head back against the chair. The numbing warmth of the liquor traveled throughout her body.

◆ ◆ ◆

How long had she known Crystal? It seemed like forever. So long that she could hardly remember what it was like not to know Crystal. The summer before Marta started college, she received her roommate assignment. At the college's suggestion, she wrote a note about herself and sent it off to Crystal Rutherford of Oakbrook, Illinois. "Dear Crystal," the letter began, "I'm very excited about starting college. I'm unsure what my major will be, but I'm leaning toward teaching and/or design. I also like to sew, bike, and read in my spare time." Marta went on to tell about her family and how she had decided on the University of Iowa for her college education. She enclosed her high school graduation photo and signed it: "Look forward to meeting you, Marta."

She received a response two weeks later. Crystal opened her letter with, "Hello roomie! I've never picked up a needle and thread in my life (and don't plan to), biking would be okay if we don't get too sweaty—but, I do like to read! *Cosmo* and *Glamour* are my favs! I like to shop, shop, and shop! Oh, and I like to try out new hairstyles—we can work on yours—it will be fun! I know what I'm going to major in—BOYS! I chose this school because my parents wanted me to experience country life. How dull is that?! But, I plan on making the best of it." Then Crystal signed off with: "Tootles! Crystal."

The letter was bad enough, but when Marta saw the photo Crystal enclosed of herself, she nearly keeled over. Marta was inconsolably depressed right up to the day she left for school.

Perhaps because Marta expected the worst, she ended up being pleasantly surprised. Crystal turned out to be a pretty decent roommate. She kept things neat and clean, she didn't snore, and she didn't try to pretend to be something she wasn't. Crystal was Crystal. Crystal liked Crystal. And, in time, Marta grew to like Crystal, most of the time.

Crystal immediately attached herself to Marta without a second thought. "Well roomie," she'd say, "What are we doing tonight?" Or, "Hey roomie, let's go get a bite to eat." Or, "C'mon roomie, we're going shopping!" And they would. Crystal covered everything. Cost was no object. If Crystal wanted to do it, she did it—and expected Marta to join her. In the beginning, Marta felt a little guilty about spending all of Crystal's parent's money, but Crystal didn't. You can't take it with you, she'd say. After all, her parents had more money than most small countries. And, frankly, Marta enjoyed it. Crystal was fun.

However, eventually Marta started to feel smothered by Crystal's constant presence. She began spending more time at the library, and when Crystal found her there, Marta started searching out other places she could procure some privacy. If Crystal noticed Marta was avoiding her, she never let on, she only complained. "Why did you take such a heavy class load this semester?" she'd squawk. Or, "All you do is study and there's no time for fun," she'd whine.

Marta hoped that eventually Crystal would find another playmate. After all, Crystal was like a celebrity around campus. She was rich, beautiful, and she always picked up the bill. Men swarmed around Crystal and the lonely female coeds who followed her were happy to have a shot at Crystal's castoffs.

While Crystal did spend some time with her ever available reserve of groupies, it only made her more petulant. "It's not the same," she'd gripe. "We're roomies, we belong together!" And again, she'd come searching for Marta. She even enlisted the help of her idolizing fans. It turned into a game of cat and mouse. And that's how Marta met Bill.

Marta found her safe haven in the fourth floor waiting room of the University hospital. Bill was an intern. Marta fell for him the minute she saw him. She planned her escapes to fit with Bill's schedule. They got to know each other. They got to like each other. Marta was on cloud nine. At the end of the semester, Bill invited her to a party on campus.

That afternoon, Marta skipped her last class and hurried to the dorm to get herself ready. She hadn't mentioned anything about Bill to Crystal—and didn't plan to. She definitely didn't want Crystal tagging along. In Marta's experience, when Crystal was around, Marta became invisible, especially to men.

Unfortunately, just as Marta was about to make her getaway unnoticed, Crystal walked through the door. "Roomie!" Crystal exclaimed and gave Marta a hug. "What are we doing tonight?"

Marta shrugged, unable to speak.

"You look fabulous! We must be going out! Well, it's about time. Thank God this semester's over. I was so lonely without my roomie! Hang on, I'll get dressed."

Marta's stomach churned while she watched Crystal throw herself together. There was nothing she could do. Bill would have to meet Crystal sometime, Marta supposed. And it was probably best to get it over with sooner rather than later. Perhaps Bill would be different. Marta knew that he already liked her, maybe that would be enough.

When they arrived at the party, Bill spotted Marta immediately. He greeted her warmly, and then, as Marta had feared, turned his attention to Crystal—all evening. Marta was despondent. She took her drink and sat in the corner, waiting, but neither of them looked her way. After some time, she slipped out the door and headed home.

Crystal returned to the dorm after midnight. She flipped on the lights and shook Marta awake. "How could you leave without me?" she admonished. "I almost had to walk home by myself."

Bill was only the first of several men Marta lost to Crystal. It wasn't that Crystal set out to do so. In fact, Crystal didn't do anything. She didn't have to. Crystal was a male magnet. One look was all it took. No man could resist her.

But, that was before Garrett Holt.

Chapter 6

Isaac opened the door to find Claudia on hands and knees cleaning up a broken vase.

"Watch your step," she cautioned.

"What happened?" Isaac asked.

She sat back on her calves. "Someone put Walter's bone on the entryway table and Walter wanted it."

Walter was their mixed breed, sixty-pound, one-year-old, knucklehead of a dog. Walter, who usually greeted Isaac with overflowing enthusiasm, peered around the corner sheepishly. He entered the area with his tail between his legs.

"Out you scoundrel!" Claudia commanded. Walter sat. His head hung down and his guilty eyes shifted back and forth between Isaac and Claudia. "Fortunately for Walter,

I didn't care too much for this vase and will look forward to shopping for a replacement."

Isaac laughed. "Let me clean this up. You go get ready."

"Twist my arm," she said, as she stood and gave him a wink. "Thanks, honey." She backed slowly into the kitchen past Walter and growled at him. He dropped to the floor and covered his head with a paw.

Isaac laughed louder. He pointed his finger at Walter. "You're trouble."

Walter's tail swished back and forth and he looked hopefully at Isaac. Usually Walter would get treats upon Isaac's return home from work.

"Don't even think about it," Isaac said. "You go on now."

Walter slinked back out of the entryway.

Isaac removed his coat, hung it on the doorknob, dropped to his knees and started picking up the pieces of glass. He got all he could see, and then pulled out the vacuum and thoroughly sucked up the rest.

He entered the kitchen and spotted his three children in the adjacent family room strewn across the furnishings fully engrossed in a rerun of *The Fresh Prince of Bel-Air.*

"Hey kids," he called in greeting.

"Daddy!" Isabelle exclaimed. She jumped up, ran towards him, and leapt into his arms. She gave him a big hug and looked up at him with her big brown eyes. "Walter didn't mean to break the vase," she said.

"I know, sweetie."

She smiled and put her hands to his cheeks feeling his five o'clock shadow. He carried her into the family room.

All eyes were glued to the television watching Will Smith get into trouble with Uncle Phil again. "Hey kids," he said again.

"Hi Dad," Avery and Jacob said in unison without turning their heads away from the television set.

"Who put Walter's bone on the entry table?" No response. "Avery? Jacob?" They both turned and stared blankly at him. "Isabelle?"

She shook her head. "No, daddy."

He sighed and set her down. She scampered back to her seat in front of the television. Their adorable third child, a spitting image of her mother. The unplanned product of their love, arriving five years after they thought their family was complete. A surprise which, he hated to admit, at first seemed burdensome, but turned out to be a blessing. Whether his other two children would admit this out loud was doubtful, but he knew they felt the same. Avery, their first born, was much like Isaac. Strong-headed and no-nonsense. Fortunately, she also got her mother's intelligence. As a stellar student she excelled at everything she tried. Jacob, at ten, was the family comedian. Avery's opposite, Jacob took nothing seriously and got tremendous enjoyment out of goading his older sister.

Isaac heard Claudia's heels on the tile floor and turned around. She stopped and struck a pose. "Wow!" he exclaimed.

"You like it?"

"Very much."

"I got it just for the occasion."

"For the occasion, or for me?" Isaac winked.

"Both." She smiled and lifted her eyebrows seductively. He started toward her, but she stiff-armed him. "Now go get ready. The babysitter will be here any minute."

"Babysitter? What about Avery?"

"She has another engagement. The Hedbergs reserved her a month ago."

"I thought we had a standing arrangement."

"They asked first. And, you know, she wants to make money. Do you want to pay her for babysitting?"

"No, it's part of contributing to the family."

"Well, she's been 'contributing' a lot lately," Claudia said. "Besides, it's good for her to experience working for others."

Isaac gave this some thought. They certainly did depend on Avery quite a bit and he knew she had to give up various events and other opportunities to make money in the past. *How was she always right?* "I suppose you're right."

She smiled. "Don't worry, I found us a sitter. Now go get changed."

Fifteen minutes later, Isaac came down to find Claudia serving up fresh ziti to their three kids and Brandi, the babysitter. "Hello, Brandi," he said.

She looked up at him through her straight, black bangs and black rimmed eyes. "Mr. Scott," she said. He noticed she had developed a bit of a lisp with the addition of the tongue ring.

Claudia continued with her instructions. "Isabelle should go to bed by 8:30 p.m., and Jacob by 9:00 p.m.

Walter will need to go out at least once tonight. Jake, you see to that."

"Okay," Jacob replied.

"Okay," she said, as she put the ziti casserole in the refrigerator. "We're on our way."

◆◆◆

Isaac and Claudia got into the car. "Brandi?" Isaac exclaimed. "You could only get Brandi?" He hit the button to open the garage door.

"Yes, she was the only one available on Valentine's Day," Claudia said.

"But, Brandi? Geez, even I'm afraid of her."

"It will be fine. Let's go."

Isaac backed out of the driveway. "I think I saw her mug shot up at the station." He put the car in drive and headed down the block, the frozen icy coating on the road crunching under the tires.

"That's impossible. She's only 16. You couldn't have." Claudia pushed the button for the seat warmer. "Don't worry, I didn't leave any cash laying around and Walter broke the only valuable thing we own."

Isaac took the ramp and merged with the oncoming traffic. Large, puffy snowflakes began to fall onto the windshield. He switched on the wipers and turned up the defroster. They moved down the highway, the snowflakes spiraling out before them making it appear as if they were moving at warp speed in a *Star Trek* movie. "Speaking of criminals, I tried, but I couldn't get anyone to fess up about putting Walter's bone on the table."

Claudia crinkled up her nose. "That's because I did it," she admitted. "I heard you vacuuming downstairs, and that made me remember that I set the bone up there when I vacuumed that very same rug this morning. So sorry, I totally forgot."

"*You* did it?" Isaac gasped.

She looked at him sheepishly. "Well, the telephone rang and I got… distracted."

"Really? Now how do I know that you didn't do it on purpose just so you could get a new vase?"

"Oh stop." She slapped his arm playfully. "I should have known better than to put it there."

He turned into the parking ramp and took a ticket. "And here I'm worried about Brandi, while my own wife is scheming a way to get a new vase."

They hustled down the street to the restaurant entrance on the corner and got out of the cold, arriving at the restaurant just in time for their 7:00 p.m. reservation. Isaac led Claudia to the elevator and they rode to the rooftop. The rooftop had been fully enclosed in glass so that even in the dead of winter, one can feel like they are dining outside. A perfect place to rid yourself, at least temporarily, of the Minnesota cabin fever that sets in after several months of being confined indoors during the inclement winter weather. The rooftop provides a lovely, open view of the city lights, but no heavy coats, hats, gloves and the like are needed.

The sun sat just below the horizon leaving a pink glow as a backdrop to the Minneapolis skyline, the moon and stars just becoming visible. The maître d' showed them to their table and handed them menus. Isaac patted his pocket to make sure the box was there. He pulled out Claudia's seat and then took the seat across the table.

"This place is spectacular!" Claudia exclaimed. "It's like being outside in the middle of the winter—but warm!"

"I thought you'd like it."

"Look!" She pointed toward the glass ceiling. "You can see the stars!"

Even though he had planned to surprise her over dessert, Isaac couldn't wait. He pulled the little box from his pocket and, with anticipation, slid it across the table.

"Isaac," she said. "What did you do? I thought we agreed to no gifts."

"This isn't a gift. Just a token of my appreciation for you." He touched her cheek. "I love you, Claudia."

Her hand went to her heart. "Oh, Isaac."

"This is for all you do for our family—taking care of the kids, cleaning the house, cooking our meals, and all those thankless jobs. You do it all so selflessly. I want you to have a symbol of how much you are appreciated. Not just on Valentine's Day, but every day." Claudia kept him grounded and made him realize what was truly important in life. With all the ugliness he witnessed day in and day out, she reminded him of life's beauty—the beauty of love, family, and faith. He got up every morning to face the world because of her. "Open it," he urged.

She pulled the box toward her and untied the red ribbon. He couldn't wait to see her reaction. She opened the box and tears welled up in her eyes. "Oh, Isaac, it's beautiful."

"Please, put it on." He smiled.

She removed it from the velvet case and slipped it on her finger. "It's perfect." A tear slid down her cheek. "But, I don't know how I can accept it with what I have to tell you."

"What you have to tell me?" he asked, suddenly alarmed. "What is it?"

"Judy called."

"As in Chandler Whitney's Judy?"

"Yes."

This was nothing new. Judy had called numerous times since Claudia had left her job there to stay home and raise their children. "Again?"

"Well yes, but this time she's offering me flexible hours, on my terms. She said they really *needed my talents*." She made finger quotation marks around the words 'needed my talents.' "Can you believe that?" She paused, unable to suppress a smile. "She said I could be reinstated as a partner within a year—even with the shortened hours."

Isaac nodded. He could feel her excitement.

"Isaac, I'd like to take it. The kids are all in school now, and I have more time on my hands than I need. Honestly, I'm bored. With the flexible hours, I know I can be there for the kids when they're home, which you know, is very important to me, as I know it is to you. And while the house may not stay as clean, and I may not be able to make the dinners you're used to, I'd really like to get back to work. To do what I trained so long and hard to do." She leaned toward him and reached for his hand. "I know you like having me home and I don't want to disappoint you." She looked down at the ring on her finger. The ring symbolizing his appreciation of her being a stay-at-home mom. "But this really is a good opportunity for me." She looked him directly in the eyes. "So, tell me, *honestly*, what do you think?"

Isaac smiled wide. "Go for it, counselor."

Her eyes lit up and she sat up straight. "Really? It's okay with you?"

"More than okay. I can see how happy this makes you. Go for it."

She grinned, jumped out of her chair and gave him a hug. "You are the best!"

◆ ◆ ◆

Blake lay wide-eyed in the dark haunted by his own visions of the past. Visions so real, so clear, so vivid, that he felt as if he were reliving them all over again.

It was in May of last year when he and Marta were invited to Crystal and Garrett's for dinner, the last time the four of them were together, and the last time he saw Garrett Holt.

The warmer spring weather had finally arrived and it was time to open the windows and let the fresh breeze blow out the stale winter air; time for plants to sprout into the warm sunshine; time to put coats into storage; time to wear short sleeves; time to buy ice cream cones; and the time for barbecues. Marta and Crystal were in the kitchen finishing up dinner preparations while Blake and Garrett minded the grill.

Garrett flipped the hamburgers and guzzled the last of his beer. "I gotta go get another. Need anything?"

"No. I'm fine, thanks."

Garrett disappeared into the house through the sliding glass door that opened to the deck. Blake checked on the burgers again, silently willing them to cook faster so that the evening could end as soon as possible. Crystal was Marta's friend, but Garrett was not his. He eyed the knobs, tempted to increase the heat, when Garrett stepped back onto the deck. He had a beer in one hand and held the other hand behind his back.

"Wanna see my new toy?"

"Another new toy, Garrett?" Blake dropped down into his lawn chair. *Here we go again.* Garrett always had a new and usually frivolous purchase he brought out to show off. The big oaf couldn't even hold down a job for more than a month at a time and he spent money like there was no tomorrow. Was it jealousy he felt? No, not really, just plain disgust. He suppressed a yawn. "What is it this time? The very latest in incredibly expensive gadgetry, I'm sure."

"Better."

"Better?"

"Better." Garrett pulled his hand from behind his back and revealed a handgun.

Blake's stomach tightened. Garrett with a gun. He felt his blood pressure shoot up like a rocket. "Whoa! Watch where you point that thing!"

Garrett aimed at the geranium planter on the corner of the deck. "Bang!" he shouted. "This 'thing' is a .45 calibur M1911A1, accurate from twenty yards, and up close, it shreds whatever it hits to bits. What do you think of that?"

Blake cringed.

"Here, just feel the power in your hands."

"No, that's okay. I don't really ..."

"Geez, don't be a sissy. Take the gun."

He laid the gun in Blake's reluctant hand.

"C'mon Blake, you're never going to stop an intruder like that. Grab the handle."

Blake grasped the handle keeping the barrel pointed toward the floor.

"There you go. Now aim it at something."

Blake eyed Garrett.

"That planter over there. Aim at that," he directed. Look down the sight. Got it lined up?"

"Yep."

"One pull and that thing would be blown to smithereens. Cool, huh?"

"Messy."

Garrett threw his head back and laughed. "No shit— one big fuckin' mess." He snatched the gun from Blake's fingers.

Blake wiped his palms on his trousers.

"Some asshole tries to break into my house—he'll be eating lead."

Blake watched him aim at nothing in particular like a kid playing cops and robbers. He shook his head. They should require an IQ test before issuing gun permits. "Just a thought, Garrett, do you know how to use that thing?"

"Of course I know how to use it. Nothing to it. Just pull this back like so and kablooey!" He raised his right eyebrow. "Should we try it out?"

"It's loaded?"

"Well, yea-ah," he said condescendingly. "What good is an unloaded gun? Wanna give it a go?"

"No. Definitely not."

"Aw, c'mon, Blake. Let's see what this baby can do." His eyes darted back and forth and he stepped over to the railing. He looked into the yard and called, "Here kitty, kitty!"

Blake rose to his feet. "Not funny, Garrett."

"Where is that damn cat? Here kitty, kitty!"

Crystal appeared in the doorway. Her hair was haphazardly pulled back and secured with a clip. She dried her hands on the apron tied around her waist. "Garrett, what are you doing? I told you to keep that thing locked up!"

He turned, with a look of disgust. "Why does everyone call it 'that thing'? It's a gun for Christ's sake. A .45 calibur M1911A1 —the finest handgun ever made."

Crystal moved toward him. "Put it away!"

He glared at her defiantly. Suddenly, a streak of black quickly ascended the stairway and headed for the deck door. "Ah, there he is!" he whispered.

"Garrett, what are you doing?" She reached out to bat his arm down but he pulled away.

The cat stood, nose to glass, waiting to be let in.

Garrett cocked the gun and aimed.

"Stop it, damn it! That's not funny!" Crystal stomped to the door, picked up the cat and tossed him inside. "PUT IT AWAY! NOW!"

Garrett looked over his shoulder with the gun still in firing position. "Hey Blake, bet your wife isn't such a bitch."

"You better put it away, Garrett."

Blake pulled the pillow over his ears and rolled onto his side, hugging his head. *What would happen now?* Nothing good, that was for sure. He rolled back over letting his arms fall to his sides and stared up at the ceiling. What would he have done to change it? Anything. He would have done anything.

Chapter 7

Isaac took the ramp and merged with the oncoming traffic, heading home. Claudia reached over, turned on the radio and started singing along to "Best of My Love" with the Emotions. In honor of Valentine's Day, KMPL was playing twelve hours of love songs, and Claudia loved love songs. For Isaac, on the other hand, it was twelve relentless hours of syrupy sweetness—more than enough to make any man go mad.

The song ended and the DJ came on with the news and weather. "It's a great night for cuddling," she said. "Temps will drop into single digits overnight. The sun thankfully returns tomorrow and we're in for a heat wave over the next few days with a high above freezing and into the mid-thirties. On a sad note, police found a gunshot victim in a home on the 4400 block of Willow Lane in

Minneapolis. Anyone with information is encouraged to contact the Minneapolis Police Department."

Claudia looked at Isaac. "Was that on your agenda today?"

Isaac nodded.

"I'm sorry to hear that." She reached over and rubbed his shoulder.

They came to a stop at the traffic light. "Yeah, thanks," he replied, as his thoughts wandered back to the day's events and the beauty who had lost her life. He looked over at Claudia. "If you were a beautiful woman . . ."

"If?" Claudia asked.

"Let me rephrase that. *Since* you are a beautiful woman, perhaps you can give me some insight."

She smiled. "That's better."

"*As* a beautiful woman, if you were going to kill yourself, how would you do it?"

"Odd question. Why do you ask?"

"The female victim, who appeared to take great pride in her appearance, died from a gunshot wound to her head. There are those, namely Vick, who think it might have been a suicide, but it just doesn't make sense to me."

"Ah, Vick." Claudia nodded. "Vick will always grasp the easiest explanation so as not to disrupt his meaningless social life."

Isaac grimaced. "Not always," he said in Vick's defense. *But sometimes it certainly did feel that way*, he admitted to himself.

Claudia rolled her eyes.

"Anyway," Isaac continued, "Unlike Vick, I have a different feeling about this one. We found another injured woman at the scene, so it seems to me there's certainly more to this story. I'm just wondering if you think the decedent's vanity would keep her from taking her life that way? That perhaps she would take pills like Marilyn Monroe or something less destructive."

"The gun was found in her hand?"

"Yes."

"No suicide note?"

"No."

"No signs of forced entry?"

"No, but we found the door to the home left wide open."

"In February?"

Isaac nodded.

"Any signs of a struggle?"

"Nothing knocked over, but things were amiss in the bedroom where we found her and there was a broken mug in the kitchen sink."

"Could that be the normal state of affairs?"

"Unknown. But I'll talk to the housekeeper tomorrow."

"Hmmm," Claudia pondered for a moment. "Well, it *is* Valentine's Day."

"What does that have to do with it?"

"Valentine's Day is one of the top holidays that triggers depression. People feel alone, sad, hopeless," she explained. "In the end, I guess if a person is depressed enough to want to end their own life, a shot to the head is the quickest way to accomplish the task. What happened to the other victim?"

"Looks like a blow to the head with a frying pan."

"A frying pan? Now that is strange. Why would a perpetrator use a frying pan to injure one and a gun to shoot the other?"

Isaac pulled into the garage and shut off the car. "Good question." He decided not to offer Vick's explanation, and added, "Let me know if you have any ideas."

All was quiet when they entered the house. Brandi was watching an episode of *Walking Dead* with Walter curled up on the couch beside her. Walter jumped down and greeted them as if they were angels descended from heaven.

"Hi Brandi," Claudia said. "How did everything go tonight?"

"Fine," Brandi responded in monotone. She clicked off the television, stood and skulked to the closet to get her coat.

Isaac and Claudia exchanged looks. "Great," Claudia replied with too much enthusiasm. "Mr. Scott will see you home."

Brandi put on her coat and stood waiting while Isaac pulled the cash from his wallet. "Here you go," he said, and handed her the money. She shoved it in her pocket with no response and opened the front door. She and Isaac headed down the block and he watched as she walked up the path to her home three doors down.

"Thanks," he called out.

"Sure," she said.

Minutes later, Isaac entered their bedroom and saw that the dress Claudia wore this evening was not the only new garment she had purchased. He smiled.

"See," Claudia said. "Everything went fine. I can report that all of our children are soundly asleep in their beds."

"Yeah, but she probably sucked the life out of them and we'll wake to find that they're zombies." He moved toward her.

"Oh stop. What I see is an awkward teenager trying to fit in somewhere."

He put his hands around her waist and kissed her neck. "Fit in somewhere? Yeah, like Hades, maybe."

"Oh right, and when you were her age you probably did things that were way more dangerous."

He kissed her lips. "I'll tell you what's dangerous, darling, is you wearing that lingerie." He smiled seductively.

Chapter 8

Isaac entered the meeting room to find Red, head down, at the table. Isaac tossed his folder onto the table and slid it across to hit the arm cradling Red's head.

"Hey," Red grunted. "Trying to get some rest here." He let out a yawn, not bothering to cover his mouth with his hand.

"How'd the surveillance go?"

Red ran his hands through his flaming curls, then crossed them behind his head and sat back in the chair. "That poor, bereaved soul didn't leave the casino 'til 2:00 a.m.," he said contemptuously. "Actually hit it big once, then lost it all. Twitchy, really twitchy." He scratched the back of his neck, stretched his arms, and then leaned forward. He fixed his eyes on Isaac's. "Something's going on there. Something big."

"Agreed," Isaac said.

Captain Petruco pushed through the door, stopped abruptly and stared at them. He looked like a vulture. Swarthy, close-set eyes, large pointed beak and hunched shoulders. He walked head first, and when agitated, his feet could barely keep up. "Where's Vick?" he asked.

Isaac shrugged.

"Haven't seen him," Red said.

Petruco sucked air in through his nostrils and his eyes bulged. "I expect you all to be here on time!" Petruco berated. "Is that understood?"

"But we *are* here, Captain," Red pointed out.

Petruco looked back and forth between Isaac and Red. "Right. But where's Vick?" he repeated.

Red held up his hands in exasperation and looked to Isaac.

Isaac stood and pulled out a chair. He'd gotten skilled at coddling Petruco over the years. "Have a seat, Captain. We can get started without him."

Petruco sat down. "Damn right. We'll get started. I don't have all day to wait around." He slapped his palms on the table. His bird eyes scrutinized each of them. "What da ya got?"

Red began. "One female dead from a gunshot wound to the head. One female struck on the back of the head."

"I know all that," Petruco derided, rolling his eyes. "The whole world knows all that, thanks to the media." He turned his attention to Isaac. "The evidence. What's the evidence so far?"

Reproached, Red sat back in his chair, his complexion turning as red as his hair.

Isaac had spent the early morning hours going through all the reports. He opened up his folder. "Not much so far, Captain. We're still waiting on the forensics and—"

The door swung open and stopped Isaac mid-sentence. Vick walked in looking as smug as a teenager. "Hey men. Sorry I'm late." He flashed a big grin. "Let's just say I left her wanting more."

Petruco let out a lecherous cackle. "That's how it's done, son!" He gave Vick a high five. "Take a seat." He slapped the chair at his right. "We just got started."

Isaac and Red exchanged a look.

Red scratched his chin. *What was it about Vick, that he always got a pass for his bad behavior? With men, and especially with women.*

Isaac looked at Vick and couldn't help but wonder, left her wanting more what? Substance? Compassion? Respect?

Vick took the seat and winked at Isaac. "Sorry for the interruption, partner. Please proceed." Vick yielded the floor with a nod.

"Thank you," Isaac responded, because it was the polite thing to do. "As I was saying, there's not much so far." He put down his pen and looked at Vick. "And we're still waiting on Vick's report. Vick? Did you bring it?"

Vick threw up his hands. "Didn't have time to get it done. I was a little tied up last night." He threw an elbow and a wink at Petruco and got a snicker in response. "But I'll have it ready later this morning. Nothing to report, really. No one was home in the neighborhood, so no one saw anything."

Nothing to report? Isaac thought incredulously. "Any comments about the couple? Rumors? Quirks? Did Crystal have any enemies?"

Vick shook his head. "Surprisingly little about the deceased—except the obvious."

"The obvious?" Petruco asked.

"Oh." Vick raised his eyebrows. "Haven't you heard?"

"No." Petruco replied.

Vick grinned. "She was hot." He leaned toward Petruco as if sharing a secret. "I mean *really* hot."

Petruco's bird head cocked sideways. "Pass 'em over," Petruco directed, and pointed at the file.

Isaac slid the file across the table. Petruco opened it and started paging through the photos, but crime scene photos were never flattering and he closed it momentarily. Getting back to the business at hand, Petruco asked, "How does this affect our case?"

"Don't know that it does, really. But you can see why jealousy was the recurring theme among the ladies of the neighborhood," Vick said. "Although none of them actually admitted it. I think 'friendly, but needy' and 'a bit self-centered,' were the main descriptors used. And no one liked her husband. Various people described him as crass, stupid, dense and the like."

Isaac was disappointed with Vick. They had worked together on several cases, but he was starting to believe that maybe Claudia was right. Vick wasn't going to let anything disrupt his shallow social life. Even a murder investigation. "That should all be in your report, Vick."

"You can depend on it, partner. All the snide, useless minutiae will be included."

Isaac turned his attention to Petruco. "I spoke briefly with the neighbor down the block, who was the deceased's college roommate, and her husband, but they were too distraught to talk immediately after receiving the news. I hope to speak with them again in the next few days. Perhaps they will be able to give us more insight on the couple."

"Well, I can give you a little insight into the deceased's husband," Red chimed in. "All those descriptors Vick mentioned fit him perfectly. Big, ignorant dude. I tailed him to Mystic Lake where he took a call that made him very nervous, and then *he* made a threatening call to someone else."

"Why didn't you tell me that in the beginning?" Petruco chided. He slid the file back across the table to Isaac, then focused in on Red. "You heard both calls?"

Red shook his head. "Not all the words, too much clanging from the slot machines. But what I did hear was all about money." He held up all the fingers on both hands. "Ten grand. Sounded like some extortion going on to me. And let me tell you what else I heard him say." Now that he had Petruco's undivided attention, he paused for effect, then announced, "He said, 'she's dead.'"

Petruco stuck out his beak. "What are you saying? That it was a hit?"

"Sure sounded like it to me," Red said.

Vick sat back in his seat. "Oh, come on. You're overplaying the significance of that statement. He could have been calling a friend to let them know of his wife's passing."

Red shook his head adamantly. "Well, whoever he was talking to did not seem friendly. The big dude was scared as a mouse. And then," Red held up his palms in bafflement, "on the next call, he roared like a lion. He was mad *and* scared. And I don't have to tell you guys—that's a very scary combination. And certainly not what you would expect of a grieving husband." He looked toward Isaac and repeated. "Twitchy. Really twitchy."

"Agreed," Isaac said. "Something is definitely going on with him."

"Sounds like our killer," Petruco declared.

"No disrespect, Captain," Vick interjected. "But I think Red's making mountains out of molehills. I'm still not convinced it wasn't a suicide. Look at the facts. No forced entry. Doesn't appear to be a robbery or a rape, and the gun was found in the deceased's hand."

"What about the woman struck on the head?" Petruco asked.

"Yeah," Red chimed in sounding a bit too much like a spurned child.

"Edna Rupp, the cleaning lady," Isaac noted.

"Like I said to Isaac yesterday, it looks like they had an argument." Vick pointed toward the report. "You saw that there was a broken mug in the sink?"

All nodded.

"Well, if that isn't an indication of a heated dispute, I don't know what is," Vick said.

Isaac shook his head. "First thing," he began. "And according to the initial report, which obviously Vick has not had time to read yet, Mrs. Rupp didn't see or speak to the deceased and didn't see or hear anything before being struck from behind."

"How do you explain that, Vick?" Red asked.

"Well." Vick adjusted his perfectly starched collar. "Maybe a very distraught Crystal, determined to end her own life, heard Mrs. Rupp coming and didn't want to be interrupted. So, she knocked her out so she wouldn't interfere. I'm just saying, I wouldn't rule it out. We're all so quick to look for a killer and I'm not seeing any evidence of that. From what I'm seeing, more evidence points toward a suicide."

"Second thing," Isaac continued. "Mr. Holt admits to being there that morning. And he also admits to arguing with the decedent and breaking that mug."

Vick slapped his palms on the table. "Well, there you go. From Holt's own mouth we know they argued. I believe that it's more than possible the Holts had an argument that left poor Crystal distraught enough to kill herself."

"Or they argued and he shot her," Red mumbled.

Petruco turned his attention to Isaac. "What else do we know?"

"Crystal's calendar showed a hair appointment the day before," Isaac said. "The salon confirmed she was there. Her credit card records showed she made many purchases recently and she had booked a flight to Los Angeles for Friday." He looked directly at Vick. "Are those the actions of a woman considering suicide?"

"Maybe she was doing anything she could think of to make herself happy," Vick said. "She was in the middle of a divorce, right?" He looked to Isaac for confirmation and got a nod. "And it sounds like it was a contentious divorce."

Isaac turned to Petruco. "We'll know more about the fatal shot when the forensics come in, but until then, I feel we need to investigate this as if there was foul play."

"Absolutely," Red agreed. "There's something very suspicious going on with Garrett Holt."

"After our meeting I'm going over to the hospital to interview Mrs. Rupp and also have an interview scheduled with Mr. Holt at noon," Isaac told them.

"Good. In the meantime," Petruco pointed his finger at Vick. "No matter what your theories are, dig up all you can on Mr. Holt." The finger moved to Red. "Stay on Mr. Holt's tail." Petruco stood and shoved in his chair. "We must investigate all possibilities," he said. He turned toward Isaac. "But focus on Mr. Holt. He did it," he proclaimed.

Chapter 9

I can see your appetite is back." Marta leaned over, brushed Matthew's dark hair back and gave him a kiss on the forehead. Still warm.

Matthew nodded sleepily.

"That's a good sign," she said pulling the covers over his chest. "Just another day or two of rest and you'll be back on the ice."

"I better be." He grinned mischievously. "They can't win without me."

She smiled. "That's the spirit." She sat next to him on the bed. He looked so much like his father. More than that, he had his father's determination. "So you, mister, better get well."

"We're playing Washburn next," he said. "They're really good."

"Well, it will be a good contest then."

"Coach says we can win if we stay focused and work together as a team."

"Good advice."

"But they beat Edison."

"Oh?"

"And Edison beat us."

"Don't think about that. Just play your best game. Win or lose, if you play your best game, you can feel good about it."

"You sound like Coach."

She smiled. "I like your Coach. Sounds like a wise man."

"Will Dad take me to the game?"

"Yes, Dad will take you. As usual," she said. Tears welled in her eyes. She stood abruptly and picked up the breakfast tray.

Matt looked concerned. "You okay, Mom?"

"A-OK," she said.

"Your eyes are all watery. Are you getting sick too?"

"Oh no, these darn contact lenses are giving me some trouble today. Now you get some rest. You need to be healthy if you're going to beat Washburn."

"Okay." He rolled to his side.

"Sleep is the best medicine," she said.

She took the tray downstairs to the kitchen as the tears overflowed and rolled down her cheeks. She set the tray down and put her hands to her head. *How would she tell Matthew about Crystal?* She was like an aunt to him. She was always interested in what he was up to and lavished him with expensive gifts. He would miss her terribly. How could she ever explain how this horrible thing happened? It would change his life, as well as all their lives. Marta paced across the kitchen, the message left on Blake's cell phone running repeatedly through her head, haunting her. *What was she to do?* Nothing. She could do nothing. It was too late. No going back now as she had made her decision yesterday.

The doorbell rang and pulled her back to the present. She wiped her eyes on the kitchen towel and took a moment to compose herself. She walked to the door and peered through the eyehole. Her stomach tightened. Patty. *Shit.* She pulled the door open. The cold air blew in.

"I have soup!" Patty crossed the threshold and kicked off her shoes. "Just what this household needs." She headed toward the kitchen.

Marta followed. *No, no, no, no!* "Well, thanks Patty. You sure didn't have to."

"I wanted to." She opened Marta's refrigerator. "Hmm… where will we fit this?" She started moving things around.

"Here, Patty. I can take care of that."

"No, no – I don't want to be any trouble. Here." She set the container next to the almond milk. "Just warm it up for a few minutes in the microwave. Well, you know." She smiled. "I've been told it's the cure for whatever ails you!" She stuck out her brightly polished lower lip and held out her arms. "You've been crying. You need a hug."

She walked over and hugged Marta. "There, there, that's better. Now come over here and sit down." She pulled out a kitchen chair.

Marta resisted, "Oh no Patty, no need to take time out of your busy day, I'm sure you've got a lot to do."

"Nonsense! Nothing's more important than being right here with you. Now please, sit." She pointed as she removed her coat and draped it over the kitchen chair.

Marta reluctantly sat. *Shit.*

"There." Patty made a sad face. "How is Matt feeling?"

"Much better today."

"Is Blake here?"

"No—" Marta began, but Patty interrupted before she could explain.

"No? He's not home with you?"

"He had meetings scheduled all morning."

"And he couldn't change them to be here with you in your time of need?"

"No, no, I told him to go. It's fine. They couldn't be changed."

"Well, never mind." She waved her hand, and, as usual, the subject switched to Patty. She raised her perfectly plucked eyebrows. "If you want to talk about important meetings, I *know* about important meetings." She pulled out a chair and sat next to Marta. "My Howard had an emergency, out-of-town meeting." She rolled her eyes. "You know, that company can't seem to get anything done without him." She leaned in. "They decide, at the last minute, just like that, that he's needed in Milwaukee."

She threw up her hands. "On Valentine's Day, no less! But, I guess that's the problem with being so important." She flicked her long bleached blond hair back over her shoulders. "Now he's missed all the excitement and barely has time to talk on the phone! Well, anyway, it's a good thing I'm here. How are you holding up?"

Excitement? Marta couldn't believe it. *That's what it was to her? Did this woman have any feelings?* Tragedy would have been a more appropriate word. Life-changing tragedy. "As well as can be expected," Marta replied. "I just need some time to myself," she said, hoping Patty would take the hint.

"Of course you do! You know, that's how I feel too. It's just too much to process." Her eyes opened wide. "Imagine! Crystal murdered just right across the street. But what could we have done? It was perfectly normal for Garrett to be there." She put her hand on Marta's shoulder. "Crystal confided in me about their counseling appointments." She shook her head. "I thought it was a total waste of time right from the beginning. That man couldn't be changed. He was just a big, mean, stupid oaf. Well, I don't have to tell you that, Marta. You must have talked with Crystal about him." She looked Marta in the eye. "Couldn't you get her to stop letting him in?"

"Well I didn't..." Marta stammered.

"And if you couldn't," she went on, not waiting for an answer, "you'd think Blake could. From what I saw, he sure seemed to have a big influence on her. I mean, we *all* knew it. The way they would just sit up in the corner of the stands whispering together. Obviously they got along famously."

Marta felt like she was falling and held tight to the edge of the table.

"But no, I'm sure no one could tell *Crystal* what to do," Patty continued. "I just feel horrible I didn't befriend Crystal like she wanted. I could tell whenever we spoke that she wanted to get closer to me. I mean, we had so much in common, it only made sense. And I'm sure I would have been a good influence on her."

Marta eyed her skeptically. If only Patty knew how they made fun of her. They called her Peeping Patty. Crystal would purposely strip down to her underwear and walk around the house when she noticed the dark opening in the center of Patty's front window curtain. A sure sign Patty had the binoculars trained on the neighborhood, and in particular, Crystal's house directly across the street. Oh how they'd laugh thinking of the wild things they could do to entertain Patty. But then again, Crystal liked attention and if no one else was there, Crystal probably would talk to Patty.

"Oh, Marta! Please don't think I'm a terrible person. I wanted to be friends with Crystal. I mean, who wouldn't? But my Howard didn't want anything to do with that awful Garrett. But, Marta, can you blame him?" She shook her head. "A good man like my Howard can't be known to consort with the likes of him." She looked at Marta for confirmation. "And with her fabulous good looks she was still a bit needy, you know?" She put her hand on Marta's. "Well of course you know, you two were best friends! She always needed someone to pay her some attention." She gave Marta's hand a little squeeze. "Like Blake did."

"Like Blake did," Marta repeated. She pulled her hand away and sat back in her seat.

"Oh no. Oh my." Patty brought her hands to her face. "Have I offended you in some way? Didn't you arrange for Blake to take Crystal to the games?"

"What are you implying, Patty?"

"I'm not implying anything." She looked down into her hands and then up into Marta's eyes. "I'm just, you know, looking after a friend."

"You know Patty, I don't think this is any of your business."

"So you didn't arrange that? Well, I can see then why you're distraught. You need some tea." Patty jumped up from her seat and started opening cupboards.

"Patty, stop," Marta pleaded.

"I know it's here somewhere." Patty opened up the next cupboard door.

"No Patty, stop!" Marta directed. Then, catching herself, she softly said, "I'm sorry. I'm out of sorts and don't feel like talking right now. I just need some time alone. Please leave."

Patty pursed her lips. "You're asking me to leave?"

Marta nodded. "Yes, please leave. I need to be alone."

"Oh I hope I didn't cause you any concern about Blake and, you know, his dalliances with Crystal. I mean it's certainly nothing to be concerned about now that she's dead."

Chapter 10

Isaac turned over the engine, put the defrost on high and grabbed the scraper from the backseat. He'd only been at the station an hour and already ice covered the windshield. He pulled on his gloves and began chipping at the frozen coating from the bottom where the hot air had begun melting it from inside. He scraped a hole just large enough to peer through and took off for the hospital. A very fine mist hung in the air making everything hazy. Cars crept down the boulevard, slowed by the poor visibility and icy roads.

Isaac turned right into the parking lot and found a spot close to the hospital entrance. He locked up and hustled to the door to get out of the cold. The all too familiar odor, that sterile, sickly smell that penetrated every corner of every hospital in the world, greeted him as he stepped inside.

He identified himself at the desk and was given Edna Rupp's room number. Five minutes later he stood outside her door. "Hey Billy-boy, how'd it go last night?" Isaac asked the officer stationed on the metal folding chair outside her room.

"All quiet on the western front."

"Good." Isaac was concerned that the assailant, learning Edna was still alive, may try to come and finish the job. "Is she awake?"

"Yeah, but she has company." He stood and stretched his arms overhead. "Okay if I go get a cup of coffee and stretch my legs?"

"Sure. I'll be about ten to fifteen minutes or so."

Bill grinned. "That's what you think." He started toward the elevators.

Isaac tapped on the door frame then stepped into the room. Edna Rupp, a small woman with intense blue eyes was lying flat in the hospital bed with her head covered in bandages. A sunburst of wrinkles sprang from the outer corners of her lids and smile lines circled the sides of her mouth. A young man sat slouched on the window sill next to the bed, his feet dangling, his hands in a ball. His hair hung limp and greasy around his face. He leered distrustfully at Isaac.

"Mrs. Rupp?" Isaac asked.

She lifted her head slightly to get a look at him. "Yes?"

"I'm Detective Isaac Scott, ma'am. Do you feel up to answering a few questions?"

"Of course, detective. Come on over here and I'll tell you what I can."

The young man hopped off the ledge and crossed his arms over his chest. "Detective, huh? Are you going to catch the slimeball who did this?"

"I'll do my best," Isaac replied. "And you are?"

"This is my son, Gib," Edna said.

"Nice to meet you, Gib." Isaac extended his hand.

Gib dismissed Isaac's out-stretched hand and shook his pointer finger at him. "You get that son of a bitch, Garrett Holt, for what he did to my mother."

Isaac raised his eyebrows. "Did you see the assailant, Mrs. Rupp?" He knew the preliminary questioning stated that she hadn't.

"No, no I didn't," she replied. "That's enough now, Gib."

Gib paced in the small space. "He did it. I know he did it." He punched his fist into the palm of his other hand. "You get that son of a bitch," he repeated. Then he turned his finger toward Edna. "You tell him, Ma. Tell him about that no-good bastard."

"Now you don't know any more than I do, Gib. So just calm down and take a seat."

"I know what I know."

"Sit, child. I'm sure the detective will get to the bottom of it."

Gib glared at Isaac. "Garrett Holt—he's the one you want. You better make him pay for what he did to her," he said then he stomped out of the room.

Edna patted the side of the bed. "Come on over here detective, where I can see you. Never mind Gib— he's got his daddy's temperament. Flies off the handle like that sometimes. Always has. A challenge, that one." She adjusted her position under the white linens. "He's my nephew's boy, actually. I adopted him after his mama ran off and his daddy drank himself to death." She let out a long sigh. "He's been with me thirteen years now— like one of my own, really." She smiled up at him. "I was blessed with two daughters, you know, but I always wanted a son. So, there you go." She reached for Isaac's hand. Her eyes twinkled. "My, my, what large hands you have. Let me see the other." Isaac held it out for her. "Married are you?"

"Yes, ma'am."

"Lean down here closer to me. I can't see so good with these old specs. The others got bent up pretty good when I fell, you know." Isaac bent down closer. She squinted, her pale blue eyes almost lost beneath the folds of her droopy eyelids. She inspected his face. "I can tell she's a good woman just by the look of you." She gave his hand a squeeze. "She takes good care of you I'll bet."

"Yes ma'am. For almost fifteen years now."

"I knew it." She released his hand. "You can straighten up now." She took note of his mid-section. "She's a good cook, too."

"Yes, she is."

"Yes she is," she repeated. "How many children you got?"

"Three. One boy, two girls. Just like you."

"Fine. That's fine." She grinned, the creases in her soft face radiating from the corners of her mouth. "You're a lucky man."

"I am indeed."

She nodded. "Well now, pull up a chair and take a seat. Let's get down to it."

Isaac draped his coat over the back of the visitor's chair and did as he was told.

"I'm afraid I won't be much help. Took a pretty good knock on the head you know."

"How are you feeling now?" Isaac pulled the chair closer.

"I'm alright, I guess. They'll keep me here today I reckon, then they'll boot me out of here to fend for myself." She winked at him. "But that's okay by me. I much prefer caring for myself. Never much liked having people doting over me—makes me nervous—like they think I'm getting old or something."

"No."

"I don't know what I can tell you 'bout all that, I went over to do the cleaning—let myself in—I know the garage combination, you know. Came up the stairs and the next thing I know, I woke up on the hallway floor with a ringing in my ears to beat the band. Don't remember anything else a'tol."

"Had you been working for Crystal for a while?"

"Oh my, yes. Pretty near four years now."

"How often did you go to clean?"

"Once a week. Unless she had a wing-ding planned for the weekend. Then I'd come again to help with the set up and cooking." She lowered her voice, "Crystal wasn't much in the kitchen, you know."

"Oh?"

"Course she didn't do much entertaining anymore since Garrett left." She frowned. "And good riddance to him. He was one poor excuse for a husband." Then she smiled at Isaac. "Not like you. I can tell you know how to care for a family. Isn't that right?"

"I do my best."

"You do your best." She nodded. "Well, that Garrett." She rubbed her forehead. "I guess there isn't any nice way to say it. That Garrett was a no-good bum if you ask me. I never could understand what Crystal—God rest her soul—saw in the likes of him. Truly a shame. Just a cryin' shame."

Isaac nodded. If first impressions meant anything, he'd have to agree with Edna. 'No good bum' seemed to fit him perfectly.

"That man hunkered around the house doing nothing, and then he'd go out and Lord only knows when he'd come back. You know, I always look to find the best in people, but this one… he was worthless, just plain worthless. He'd just sit in front of that TV all day. Sports. One t'another. That's how he was. Why, Crystal had to hire someone to cut the grass! He wouldn't lift a finger." She shook her head in disgust. "A big, strong man like that—not worth a wit. Never could hold down a job. He wouldn't even take Crystal out. Imagine, a beautiful, rich wife like that and he didn't treat her any better than that old cat of theirs.

Poor thing." She reached for Isaac's hand and clasped it between her own. "Don't you let Garrett take that cat, now. He can stay with me. I'll care for him. Always did, anyway. Old Ebony, starved for affection, he sure was. Just like Crystal. Two peas in a pod, those two." She searched his face. "You've got to promise me not to let anything happen to him."

"I promise. I'll let them know that you'll take care of him."

She patted his hand. "I know you will. There's no telling what Garrett would do. Was going to use him for target practice, I hear tell, 'til Crystal snatched him up and away, thank the Lord."

Isaac raised his brows. "Was Garrett a violent man?"

"Oh pooh, he didn't seem to care about anything 'cept his sports. Crystal would yell and he'd ignore her. Sit glued to that TV. Wasn't 'til she stood right in front of it that he'd even notice her. Then he'd yell at her to get away —'get out of my face,' —he'd say. They were both so head-strong you know." She shook her head. "Oh, I suppose when Crystal would start slapping at him, he'd push her away. One time he shoved her against the hot stove. I had a pot roast cooking, and Crystal hit the kettle, burned her hand, and supper spilled all over the countertop." Edna grimaced at the memory. "Crystal was madder than a hornet. Then Garrett up and left just like that. You know, he'd take off without a word where he was going or when he'd be back. Crystal hated that more than anything."

"Tell me more about Crystal."

Edna looked toward the ceiling. "Crystal was one of a kind, you know. A walking contradiction. I never met one like her before and doubt I ever will again. This way one minute and that way t'other. Oh, nice enough—and generous with her money. But her mama and daddy spoiled her if you ask me." She turned her keen eyes toward Isaac. "She always needed someone to pay attention to her. You might think it was pure vanity, but it was insecurity too. You'd never guess that just to look at her, though. But I got to know Crystal pretty well, I guess. I did more than just clean her house, you know. I was like a mother to her. I gave her good advice, too. But then again," she sighed, "she didn't follow it much. Crystal could get somewhat high and mighty at times, but I didn't pay that no never mind. Her up-bringing caused that." Edna's blue eyes softened. "And, of course, she did have her own cross to bear."

"Oh? What was that?"

"Beauty," she said. "When you're a beauty like Crystal, people don't look at you like they look at other people. Women don't take to you and men don't care 'bout anything but the wrapping."

"Ah."

"Yes sir. It was a curse if you ask me."

"Had Crystal been upset about anything lately?"

"Well now, no—and that's the saddest part. There just isn't any understanding it, is there?"

"What's that?"

"Everything was working out just grand. Crystal finally got the gumption to kick that bum out." Edna adjusted the bandage on her head and tucked in the little wisps of hair sticking out around the edges. "Just like I told her to, you know." She held up her finger toward the ceiling. "I'd say, Crystal, send him packing and find yourself a family man. There's lots of apples on the tree. This one's rotten. Chuck it and pick another." She smiled at Isaac. "Well, glory be, she finally took my advice. Garrett was gone. And," She paused and raised her eyebrows. "Crystal had a new beau. She didn't exactly tell me that, you understand. But when you care for a person the way I cared for Crystal, you just know."

Isaac imagined that was more than likely so.

"I could tell this one was a nice fella too, just from the look on her face."

The hospital cart squeaked and caused Isaac to turn. A bright faced girl in white pushed the cart to the foot of the bed. "Excuse me!" the nurse said. "Time to take Edna's vitals!" She leaned toward Isaac. "She probably should get some rest too."

"I understand," he said. "Well Edna, I guess I better be going. It was a pleasure talking with you."

"Oh my dear, it was *my* pleasure, detective." Her eyes twinkled. "I like you. You have a nice smile. And you're a good listener, too. You come visit me when I'm all settled in at home. We'll chat some more."

Isaac gently squeezed her hand. "I'd like that."

Chapter 11

Marta stared out the front window down Willow Lane. Willow Lane where she and Blake bought their first house. Willow Lane where they had planned to raise their son. Willow Lane where there wasn't a single willow tree to be found. The best she could figure was that they had cut them all down when developing the property and the name had been given in their memory.

Frost now covered the yellow tape surrounding Crystal's house. Everything was still and frozen. The trees lining the road looked almost plastic because of the coating of ice on their trunks and branches. She watched as Howard's car backed out of the driveway. *Poor Howard,* she thought, *always off on business trips. But how else would one stay married to Patty?* Patty stuck her nose in everyone else's business and always told you her thoughts on any subject under the guise of "friendly advice." But Marta had to admit, although Patty was infuriating and insensitive, Patty had been right about one thing this morning. Blake really should have stayed home with her today. But then, how could she blame Blake when it was she herself who had encouraged him to go? She wrinkled her forehead. But why hadn't he argued? He said he had some very important business to attend to. She gulped down her last sip of coffee. *Very important business?* Wouldn't consoling your wife after her best friend's murder qualify as *most* important?

She laughed. Who would have ever thought she'd call Crystal her best friend? Had it ever been a choice? Crystal just always seemed to be there. She shook her head. And now she was gone.

She turned to fill her cup and checked her watch. He said he'd be home soon. Soon. Such a nebulous word. She picked up the phone to call him, then put the phone back down. The truth was, that she had wanted him to go. She hadn't given him a choice. But why hadn't he resisted? Tears filled her eyes as feelings of rejection took over. Sure, she had told him to go, but what she really wanted was for him to *want* to be there with her more than anything else.

She couldn't help but smirk at the irony of it, because that's exactly how Crystal felt about Garrett. For different reasons, of course. For Crystal, it was a matter of wanting what she couldn't have. Crystal was used to getting whatever she wanted, however and whenever she wanted it. But that was before she met Garrett Holt.

◆ ◆ ◆

Marta remembered Crystal and Garrett's first meeting clearly. It was on a beautiful fall day. The leaves had just begun to change and the cool breezes encouraged the wearing of sweaters. Crystal and Marta went to the Phi Kappa Gamma house to watch the Lions versus Bears football game with the large crowd that always gathered there to watch sporting events. Detroit was beating Chicago by two points with only thirty seconds left in the game. Chicago had the ball and was moving it down the field into field goal range.

As usual, over the course of the game, every fraternity member had taken their turn wooing Crystal and Crystal enjoyed their attention. Every member, that is, except the one who sat glued to the TV. So glued, he carried on a colorful private dialog with his team yelling things like 'Get your shit together!' and 'What are you, a bunch of fuckin' women?'

This started to bother Crystal. Not because of the foul language he used, or the sexist comments he made, or how loud he yelled, but because he didn't even notice that she was in the room. To Crystal, that was first, completely inconceivable, and second, absolutely unacceptable. Where was the usual admiration? Why wasn't he groveling for her favor like the others?

She set out to remedy this incomprehensible affront. Because of the football game, she believed he just hadn't had the opportunity to appreciate her beauty, so she casually strolled in front of the screen on her way to get a beer. To her surprise, this elicited an annoyed scowl from Garrett, which in turn elicited an even larger scowl from Crystal. *How dare he?* Outraged, she narrowed her eyes, and just as the ball was snapped for a field goal that, if good, would put Chicago in the lead, she stopped dead center in front of the TV, put her hands on her hips and declared, "Listen you, no one treats me that way. Apologize now."

Garrett stood, shoved her to the side, and yelled "Get out of the way, bitch!"

Crystal stumbled and fell to the floor just as the ball went wide of the goal post.

Garrett yelled "Shit!" He fell back into his chair, head in his hands. Everyone could tell he had a lot riding on a Bear's upset.

A rush of frat boys surrounded Crystal ready to console her. "Crystal, are you okay?" "Crystal let me help you." "Crystal would you like to lie down?" Crystal let the boys help her find comfort on a nearby chair while she leered at Garrett Holt.

Garrett Holt continued his rant at the TV screen oblivious to all else.

Marta watched as Crystal came apart.

On the walk home Garrett was all Crystal could talk about. "How dare he?" she exclaimed. "No one treats me like that." She couldn't fathom how a man could be more interested in a football game than in her. No male had ever dismissed Crystal the way Garrett did.

From that moment on Garrett Holt became Crystal's obsession. She managed to get his schedule and planned her every move around it, and took every chance to parade her wares in front of him, but to no avail. Crystal was despondent.

Attempting to console her, Marta said "Crystal, forget him. The only thing he cares about is sports."

And just like that, a light bulb went on in Crystal's head. "Marta, you are so right," she said.

Marta sat momentarily dumbfounded. After all the moaning and whining, that was all it took? "Yes, I am," Marta said. "It's time to change course – move on to other things."

But lo and behold, the next weekend Crystal and Garrett went to see the Vikings lose to the Green Bay Packers and they didn't miss a Vikings game the rest of the season. Home or away, they were there. At first Marta was appalled by the flagrant way Garrett used Crystal, but Crystal finally had Garrett's attention and Marta was enjoying the time to herself.

♦ ♦ ♦

Just after the Super Bowl, in early February of that same year, Crystal's wealthy, well-connected parents died in a car crash. Crystal, their only child, dropped out of college and went home to Illinois to take care of their personal business and plan the funeral. Dignitaries, statesmen and icons of the business world attended the service. And Crystal inherited a fortune.

In the evening after the funeral, Crystal and Garrett were off to the airport.

"I just want to get away," Crystal told Marta.

To Marta's horror, Crystal came back married.

"He begged me." Crystal flashed a victory grin. "Begged me," she repeated. "I turned him down three times, but then he pulled out the ring." She held out her left hand for Marta to see. It was a massive diamond surrounded by two more rows of diamonds. It had to cost a fortune. Marta gasped.

Crystal grinned again. "And I thought, now *that* belongs on my finger."

Marta looked at Crystal's beaming face. "It certainly does suit you," Marta said, while inwardly knowing this was a mistake of major proportions.

"Yes, it certainly does!" She giggled triumphantly. Clearly, Crystal felt she had won.

Marta did her best to smile. But what Marta knew, and Crystal didn't realize, was that Garrett was the booby prize. Marta took Crystal's hand to examine the ring more closely. *Garrett didn't have the funds to pay for something so extravagant,* she thought to herself. "I've never seen anything so beautiful."

"Garrett said the jewelry store salesman said I deserved a ring as beautiful as me."

Marta later found out that Garrett had charged the ring to the hotel room. Crystal had paid for her own engagement ring. Garrett Holt had been a remora from the start.

However, if it hadn't been for Garrett Holt, she may never have ended up with Blake. How she loved Blake. She would do anything for him. And, he said he'd be home soon. Just this one thing he needed to do.

◆ ◆ ◆

She opened the office door a crack and heard him say "Yes, that's correct. She's dead." He paused. "Hang on a minute." He cupped the receiver and looked at his assistant expectantly.

"You have an angry caller on line two," she whispered.

He nodded. She backed out and slid the door closed.

He returned the receiver to his ear. "No, no one will find out," he assured the caller. "I'll wait for your direction."

He pushed the button ending the call, took a breath, and pressed line two. "Blake Coburn," he said.

"Your idiot attorney friend won't give me my money," yelled the voice on the other end of the line.

"Garrett?"

"Yes, Blake, and I want you to call that poor excuse for an attorney you got Crystal involved with and tell her that I'm Crystal's husband and it's my money—not some trustee's."

"I'm sorry, Garrett," Blake began.

"Yeah well, you should be. This is all your fault. If you hadn't gotten involved, I wouldn't be in this mess. Now call that damn attorney and get this straightened out!"

"I can't do that, Garrett. It would be a conflict of interest."

"Don't give me that shit. You set this whole thing up and now I'm screwed. They tell me I need some trustee's approval to get my money."

"I'm sure Crystal just wanted to be sure you were well taken care of."

"That's bullshit! I need that money, Blake, and I need it today. Now you get on the phone and call that attorney—now!"

"I can't do that, Garrett," Blake responded evenly. *And even if I could, I wouldn't.*

"Fuck you!" Garrett slammed down the receiver.

Chapter 12

Isaac picked up the receiver on the first ring. "Hello, Counselor. How are the new digs?" After Claudia got the kids off to school, she met with Judy, signed her employment agreement, and took care of all the necessary paperwork at Chandler Whitney to get reinstated.

"Absolutely great," Claudia said. "I'm sitting here in my eighteenth floor office looking out at the Minneapolis skyline."

Isaac smiled. After all these years, nothing made him happier than knowing Claudia was happy. "Go get 'em, girl!"

"I'm on my way out to lunch with the group, but wanted to give you a head's up."

"Oh?"

"The almost ex-husband of one of our very wealthy, very recently deceased clients just stopped in regarding the client's will and left, under duress, a VERY unhappy man."

"Oh?"

"The client died yesterday from a gunshot wound to the head. I heard she was very attractive. I thought you might know who I'm talking about."

Isaac sighed. "Oh."

"We had to call building security to have this individual forcibly removed. He's big, loud and scary. The wife's attorney is quite shaken. I'm worried about you. Be careful. This person has come unglued."

"Good to know. Thanks." He hung up the phone and looked at his watch. Eleven thirty. Garrett was to arrive at noon. Isaac looked the file over one more time making note of the particular questions he had for Mr. Holt and then went looking for Vick.

◆ ◆ ◆

Isaac and Vick opened the meeting room door to find Garrett pacing the room. Vick puffed up at the sight of Garrett. He was tall and fit with classic, strong Nordic features. A threat to Vick's machismo.

"Mr. Holt," Isaac greeted him. "I'd like you to meet Detective Marchese."

Vick reached out his hand intending to show this good-looking adversary that he was the king. Garrett shook it as if Vick were a leper.

"He'll be sitting in on your interview," Isaac said. "Please have a seat."

Isaac could almost see the steam rise off Garrett as he yanked out a chair and plopped down. He glared at Isaac with contempt, "Can we please get this over with? I've got things to do today."

"I'm sure you do. There's always so much to take care of after the loss of a loved one." He searched Garrett's face for some trace of grief or guilt. "Please accept our condolences on your loss. I'm sure you are as eager as we are to find out how this tragedy happened," he said, effectively taking some of the wind out of Garrett's bluster.

"Fine. Let's get on with it," Garrett snarled and slumped back in his seat. "Although I could save us all this waste of time 'cause I don't have any information about 'how this tragedy happened.'"

"Well, we don't want to leave any stone unturned, Mr. Holt. Sometimes even the smallest details can be helpful."

Vick and Isaac took seats across the table from Garrett. Garrett faced the one-way mirror. After Claudia's call, Isaac called Red to make sure he'd be available to sit on the other side of the glass and observe in case things started to go awry.

"Okay, why don't we start with your exchange with Crystal that morning."

"Our *exchange*?" Garrett asked. "I went over there like I always do on Thursday mornings to pick her up for our counseling appointment. Only this time she wasn't ready to go." And, he did not mention, was not planning to go.

Vick stared at Garrett. *How did a beauty like Crystal Holt end up with such a lunkhead.*

Isaac couldn't find any emotion in Garrett's statement, as if yesterday was just like any other day. Go for a counseling appointment in the morning. Wife found dead that afternoon. Same old, same old. There had to be a trigger. Isaac just had to find it. "Go on," Isaac encouraged.

"So, I got myself a cup of coffee," he said in a tone of voice that sounded like the words 'you idiot' were automatically added to the end of the sentence.

Isaac inwardly groaned. He and Vick exchanged a look. It was clear they'd have to pry answers from Garrett. Vick leaned back in his seat. Isaac decided it was time to be more direct. "In our earlier conversation you said that you and she had an altercation. What lead up to that?"

"The usual." He shrugged.

"The usual?" Isaac asked. "Do your arguments often end with broken dishware?"

"No," Garrett answered defensively. But, he didn't add, she had promised she'd have the money for him, and she didn't, so he broke the mug.

"And you also mentioned that you shoved her that morning."

"She was playing with me." He shifted in his seat. "I didn't like it." Not only didn't she have the money like she promised, she cut him off. Just like that. Cut him off. *And that deserved a lot more than a little shove,* he thought to himself.

Isaac looked him directly in the eye. "She was shot with a gun that was registered to you."

"Are you accusing me?" he asked indignantly.

"Well, Mr. Holt, from all accounts you were the last one to see her alive and you are also the one who has the most to gain."

To Isaac and Vick's surprise, Garrett stood abruptly and roared, "Most to gain?"

This sudden movement startled Vick and he pushed back in his chair. He gave Isaac a wide-eyed look, then threw a glance at the mirror behind them, ready to call in the cavalry.

Isaac remained seated. *Now he was getting to him*, he thought with satisfaction. Money was always at the top of the trigger list.

"Well, yeah, you'd think so, wouldn't you?" Garrett glared at Isaac. "I AM her husband. It should all be mine." He began pacing again, his eyes were fire.

Vick inched to the edge of his seat ready to bolt for the door if things got ugly.

"But no, nooooo," Garrett snarled, the venom oozing from his lips. "Some pussy, banker, trustee gets to tell me how much of my money I can have and when I can have it. Yep, those idiot lawyers tell me that somebody at a bank who doesn't know me, doesn't know my lifestyle, and doesn't understand how I make a living, is in charge of dolling it out as he sees fit." And to emphasize the point he repeated, "As he sees fit!" He ran his hands over his short-cropped hair. "What does he know?" In answer to his own question he spewed, "He doesn't know shit!"

Isaac decided he was glad he wasn't in that banker's position and thought it might be wise to notify him to watch his back. Isaac continued with the prickly questions. "You also asked if I had the divorce papers. Were you on the verge of a divorce, Mr. Holt?"

"Divorce? Hell no. She was always threatening, but that's just Crystal," he scoffed. "She was just going through one of her moods." To prove this point he added, "She even said that morning we didn't need counseling anymore." Actually, she said she was done with counseling because it was over between the two of them, but he'd never admit that. He in turn had pleaded with her to let things get back to the way they were. He had declared again and again that he really needed her. But she had no clue just how desperately he did need her. If she had, things might have ended differently. Who would have expected *this* turn of events now that she was dead? Who would have expected that he would be in a worse situation now than he was before?

"Since your wife's money came from inheritances, you wouldn't be able to include that money in a divorce settlement," Isaac said. "That would change your financial situation substantially. Isn't that correct, Mr. Holt."

"Don't Mr. Holt, me." He pointed his finger at Isaac. "You and pretty boy here, don't know anything about our financial situation." He used air quotes around the words 'our financial situation.' "Everything was just fine, but some idiot lawyer stuck their nose in and stunk it all up," he grumbled, wishing fervently he had known about Crystal's trust before she died. "So now I don't have it."

He slapped the wall then put both hands to his head. He let out a sigh as all the wind left his sails. "I don't have it," he repeated.

Isaac watched a change come over Garrett. He could almost see the wheels turn inside Garrett's head. Garrett looked back and forth between Vick and Isaac, then sat back down at the table. "So, I guess you're going to arrest me, huh?" He held out his wrists as if he expected to be handcuffed. "Hold me in custody while you figure this out, right?"

Chapter 13

Marta sat staring into her coffee cup waiting for the sound of the garage door opening and Blake's return. She heard a thump in the room overhead. Matthew was up. He would return to school tomorrow. She stood and gazed out the window to the back yard, the trees up to their armpits in snow. She sighed. She couldn't wait any longer. She needed to tell Matthew now. She'd hate for him to hear about it on the news or from the kids at school. It needed to come from her. He would be devastated. He and Crystal had a special bond.

Was it really only three years ago since her diagnosis? Only three years ago that breast cancer relentlessly took control of their lives? It was impossible for her to describe the myriad of emotions she felt upon hearing the news. None of them good. From denial to anger to self-pity to fear to dread. She hoped to be spared the torture her mother experienced from that cruel, bloodthirsty disease. The ruthless slayer that took her mother's life at such a young age. But, Marta was one of the unlucky ones to inherit a BRCA1 mutation. It was in her genes.

When Crystal heard the news she announced that those doctors didn't know what they were talking about and flew her father's doctor in from Chicago to give Marta a second opinion. To everyone's disappointment, but expectation, his diagnosis came back the same.

Crystal showed up the next day with a beautifully wrapped package for Marta. Marta opened it and saw three lovely night gowns. The note said, "If you've got to go through this, you might as well do it in style." Marta's initial reaction was anger. Obviously Crystal had no idea what she was going through. Do it in style? Who cares about style when your life is hanging in the balance? But, then as Blake reminded her, empathy wasn't really Crystal's thing. Crystal was only doing what Crystal knew how to do to support her. Crystal showed her love with money. And by that measure, Crystal showered Marta with love throughout her ordeal. And, Marta later admitted, wearing that pretty nightie did somehow make a difference. It made her feel like she was somebody, not just a statistic.

They somberly looked at all the treatment options and, because of her family history, decided on a double mastectomy. She'd have chemotherapy before surgery to shrink the tumor, and chemotherapy afterward to kill any remaining cancer cells.

When Crystal heard Marta would probably lose her hair, she said, "You've needed a new style for a long time. It's best to start from scratch." She followed up by bringing in a wig expert. They spent hours trying on different styles and landed on one with the hairstyle she was still wearing today.

As Marta lost weight throughout treatment, Crystal exclaimed "You've dropped two sizes! Time for new skinny jeans!" The next day, Crystal showed up with three new pairs of designer jeans. And suddenly, the weight loss didn't just remind Marta of how weak she'd become.

When Marta told Crystal about the reconstructive surgery that would follow, Crystal had exclaimed, "Get rid of that belly and get two perky breasts? Sounds like a win-win to me!" She showed up the next day with a sleek black dress. "For your celebration dinner!"

While Marta and Blake spent time in the hospital, Crystal stepped in to take care of things at home. She arranged for Edna to keep their house clean and make their meals, and to their surprise, Crystal made it her top priority to care for Matthew. Prior to this time, Crystal had shown only a passing interest in Matthew, so Marta had significant doubts of her ability to care for him. But under their current circumstances, Marta didn't have a choice. And Crystal insisted. And Crystal always got her way.

To their further surprise, Crystal and Matthew got along famously. Matthew loved the way Auntie Crystal made 'artificial French toast' in the morning—toasted bread with butter and syrup (the extent of Crystal's cooking abilities), and let him have coffee. She taught him the jitter bug, took him to the zoo, the waterpark and the arcade, and introduced the preschooler to caviar. When spring arrived, Crystal had an extensive swing set-play house set up in the back yard and the two of them would spend hours there. Crystal sunning herself, and Matthew swinging and climbing like a monkey having the time of his life.

At the end of summer, just before Matthew started kindergarten, Crystal took him school shopping. She bought him school supplies, expensive new clothes, the very hippest tennis shoes, and cutting-edge hockey equipment. Once they finished shopping, Crystal took Matthew to Aveda for the latest in boy's haircuts and they ended the day with dinner at Dairy Queen. Since Marta's remission, this school shopping trip had become an annual event. One Matthew eagerly anticipated.

Marta turned from the window and started up the stairs. *How would she break the news?* She couldn't blurt out that Auntie Crystal had been murdered. No, that would never do. She had to find a softer way to tell him.

She peeked around the doorframe and saw him playing with his Nintendo games.

"Hey, Mom."

"Hey, Matt."

"What's up?"

She pulled the chair next to his bed. "Honey, I have some very sad news to tell you."

His little cherub face looked at Marta expectantly.

"Auntie Crystal is gone."

"Already?" He looked surprised. "But I thought she was going with daddy."

Marta sat back in her seat as though she'd been physically pushed. "With daddy?" she sputtered.

"Sure, to California to start a new life." He said matter-of-factly. "And I get to visit and go to Disneyland!"

Chapter 14

Twenty minutes later Isaac concluded the interview and left Garrett to wait while the three detectives met in the hallway.

"Why didn't you arrest him?" Red asked incredulously. "He's a powder keg."

"Red's right," Vick agreed.

Red gasped at Vick's endorsement. They rarely stood on the same page on anything. Red saw Vick as self-absorbed and shallow. And Vick didn't seem to even notice Red existed. Red looked over his shoulder to see if Peg was in earshot. All the ladies swooned over Vick. So this commendation could certainly boost Red's reputation. Peg sat at her desk and gave a little wave in his direction. His heart leapt. He never expected those words to come out of Vick's mouth and he sure hoped Peg heard them.

"We should arrest him," Red said with the confidence that comes when you know you're supported.

"Are you kidding me?" Isaac asked.

"Dude's crazy, man," Red responded.

"Stupid, certainly," Isaac acknowledged. "And scared."

"He should be scared," Vick said. "He killed his wife."

The forensics reports were coming in, and it was unequivocally determined that this had been a murder, not a suicide, totally invalidating Vick's theory. While Crystal's fingerprint was on the trigger, the bullet entered Crystal's head at an odd angle indicating that the gun was approximately a foot away from her head. Her hand would have been bent back against her wrist in a position that would have made it nearly impossible for her to engage the trigger on her own. The blood splatter also indicated something had covered most of Crystal's hand when the gun went off. Most likely, that something was another person's hand or hands indicating there was a struggle while the gun was in Crystal's hand. The blood splatter also showed that something human-sized blocked the splatter from reaching the area directly in front of Crystal. So, whoever shot Crystal had to be covered in that splattered blood.

Isaac sighed. Vick seemed ready to jump on the next easiest solution: the husband did it. "Maybe," Isaac acquiesced. "But let's take this one step at a time."

"We should arrest him just to keep him off the streets," Red said. "He's twitchy."

Isaac shook his head. "We don't have enough solid evidence for an arrest."

"I think you're wrong this time, partner," Vick said. "I think we've got everything we need. He certainly had the opportunity. As you said, he was the last to see her alive. He certainly seems more than capable of the deed, and his motive is obvious."

"Yeah, money," Red added unnecessarily.

Isaac pursed his lips. "I know how it looks, but it doesn't feel right. Who asks to be arrested?" he asked rhetorically. "Only someone who's more afraid of being on the outside."

"I still think he's guilty," Red grumbled.

"I think he's guilty of something too," Isaac agreed. "But I'm not sure it's his wife's murder. And if not, I also think he's our best lead to find the true killer. Putting him in jail is the last thing we should do."

During the last twenty minutes of the interview Garrett teeter-tottered between surrender and defiance. Just like a stray cat chased by a dog, he wanted the protection of a cage but not to be trapped inside. Nevertheless, and despite Garrett's bizarre behavior, Isaac extracted his alibi. Garrett said he left Crystal, alive, at the house and went directly to the gym that morning. Since he'd have to check in, they could easily confirm that. The coroner estimated the time of death to be between 9:00 a.m. and 10:00 a.m.

Isaac turned to Vick. "Vick, check out his alibi." They hadn't found any bloody clothes at or around Crystal's home or in her garbage. They had to be somewhere. Garrett Holt did not strike Isaac as the brightest bulb in the box, so if he was the killer, Isaac was sure he would have left a trail behind. "And get a search warrant for his home and the gym," he added.

Vick zipped his bomber jacket. "I think you're making a mistake, partner. He's going to run."

"Noted," Isaac responded, then he zeroed in on Red. "Red, whatever you do, don't let him out of your sight."

◆ ◆ ◆

Red headed to his car and pulled around the lot in sight of Garrett's Jaguar. While waiting for Garrett to emerge from the station, he picked up his phone and hit the speed dial button he was using more and more frequently. "Hey Peg, it's Red."

"What's up, Red?" Peg asked with that little creak in her voice he found so endearing.

"Back on surveillance and just wanted to hear a friendly voice." Full disclosure, not just *any* friendly voice, he wanted to hear *her* voice. But he couldn't tell her that.

"Funny. I'm in need of the same thing," she said.

His heart skipped a beat.

"Everyone is crazy around here. Particularly Petruco."

"Doing the vulture walk?" Red asked.

"Yes!"

"When he does that, I just want to stick out my foot and trip him. He'd drop beak first to the floor."

She laughed with a little snort.

He smiled. He could just picture her with that cute little space between her front teeth.

"Red you are hilarious."

Garrett emerged from the station and slid into his Jaguar.

"Looks like we're pulling out so I'm going to have to sign off. Thanks for talking with me."

"Always a pleasure, Red. Take care!" The line went dead. He smiled. 'A pleasure,' she had said. The smile got even bigger. *The pleasure was all his.* Red pulled out of the parking lot and stayed a few cars back, but it didn't appear Garrett worried about being tailed. He pulled into a commercial strip center off Highway 5, and Red pulled in behind. He watched as Garrett entered the coffee shop near the center.

Red pulled on his stocking cap, tucked his red locks underneath, and followed. A fake fire burned in the pot belly stove in the corner and a young student sat in one of the large upholstered chairs nearby busily typing away on her computer. The aroma of freshly brewed coffee filled the air. He spotted Garrett at the counter and stepped in behind him.

The barista stood behind the register admiring her nails. "What can I get you?" she asked Garrett without looking up. She had a different color fingernail polish on each nail, and if held flat on the table it looked like a rainbow – from purple to blue to green to yellow, orange and red.

"Tall mocha," Garrett responded.

She pulled a tall cup from the stack and a marker from the counter. "Name?"

"Bob," he said and held out a ten-dollar bill.

That got her attention. She gave Garrett a sneer. "Hi Bob." Not many paid with cash anymore and she found it kind of a hassle. It was much easier for her to send the customers through with a slide of a card. Cash required making change. She grabbed the bill from his hand, tapped the screen on the register with the green painted fingernail, and gave Garrett his change noticing that he didn't bother to drop anything in the tip jar.

Red watched as "Bob" walked to the pick-up area and stepped up to the counter. "Nice nails," he said to the barista.

"Uh huh." She looked at him impatiently.

"A tall Chai, please. For Red." He paid with a credit card and dropped a couple coins in the jar. The barista nodded at him.

Red moved in next to Garrett as they waited for their drinks. "Beautiful day!" he said in greeting to allay any suspicion that he was a police officer in pursuit of a murderer.

Garrett sneered at him.

Mission accomplished. "Whew! That storm the other day sure was something, huh?" Red commented trying to draw him in using Minnesota's unpredictable weather, always a bonding force for the state residents. With good weather, everyone rejoiced together. With bad weather, everyone commiserated with one other.

Garrett ignored him and scanned the room.

Red scanned the room as well. In addition to the young student, some middle-aged women chatted at a nearby table about an upcoming charity event, a few other students conferred about their weekly quiz results, and a business man in a suit stood and vacated a back corner booth.

"Tall mocha," the barista called. Garrett picked up his drink and headed toward the back of the shop passing the business man who left through the front door. Garrett slid into the surrendered booth. He pulled out his cell phone and took a sip of his coffee.

Red took his coffee and chose a seat near the door. He wanted to be sure Garrett didn't leave without him. Here he had a perfect view of both Garrett and his red Jag parked outside. As usual, Isaac was probably right to have Garrett followed, Red conceded. Red was certain Garrett was up to something, since he felt the need to use an alias in a coffee shop.

Red watched Garrett send a text. Then Garrett sat, phone in hand, waiting for a response.

Red discretely checked the concealed firearm in his pocket. After such a volatile and psychotic interview, Red wanted to be prepared for anything. No predicting this one. He took another scan around the room. All status quo.

He pulled out his cell phone and pretended to review messages, then decided to text Peg. He took a deep breath, and typed "Speaking of hilarious, have you seen *Plus One*?" He clicked send. His heart pounded. *Would he go through with it this time or chicken out again?*

He received an almost instantaneous response. "No, but Vick was telling me about it."

His heart sank. Vick. *How should he to respond to that?* He sighed. *Time to chicken out again,* he told himself. He typed: "Gotta run. Perp on the move," he lied.

Fifteen minutes passed. Red watched while Garrett stared at his phone and sipped his drink. Red thought he looked increasingly anxious, but maybe it was just because Red knew he should be. Garrett stood and Red readied himself to follow, but Garrett slipped through the door marked "Restroom," so he stayed put. Ten minutes passed without Garrett's return. Red shifted uncomfortably in his seat. Twelve minutes. What was taking so long? Red walked to the back and pulled open the restroom door which opened to a hallway. Panic set in. Obviously several establishments in this commercial center shared the restrooms in this hallway. He followed the arrow to the men's restroom and swung the door open. One stall was occupied. He walked casually to the sink, turned on the faucet and began washing his hands. Momentarily, a man emerged from the stall, and it was not Garrett Holt. Red grabbed a paper towel and hightailed it to the door. He searched up and down the hallway. No sign of him. The common hallway led to an exit. Red pushed through the door which opened onto an alley. Nothing. He went back into the coffee shop to check the street. Garrett's Jaguar was still there, but Garrett was not in it. *Where did he go?* His head fell to his chest. He'd lost him.

Chapter 15

Blake came into the kitchen and took Marta into his arms.

"Let's get away," he said. "Now might be the perfect time to hike the Grand Canyon."

Wouldn't that be nice, she thought, *to pretend everything was fine. To pretend they could just go on as always. To pretend that secrets will stay secrets.*

"We could camp under the stars," he continued. "Breathe fresh air and get out of this frozen state."

◆ ◆ ◆

She remembered the first time they camped together. The spring after Crystal married Garrett Holt, Marta signed up with a student group for a canoe trip to the

Boundary Waters Canoe Area Wilderness, or BWCA as it is known. The group headed by bus to Ely, Minnesota, to get outfitted. The group included seven first-time campers, and their guides, Blake Coburn and Kirsten Berry. They all gathered inside for orientation.

"We will embark on a journey together in a short time, but before we go any further, I'm going to warn you about a few things," Blake said with a devilish smile. "And give you an opportunity to back out." The group emitted some nervous laughter. "We have one requirement when camping in the BWCA," he said. "Leave no trace. Leave no trace means, when we leave a campsite there should be no evidence we were there. Glass and aluminum containers are not permitted in the BWCA. If you have any, please toss them in the recycling bins in the corner." He gestured toward the back corner of the room. All eyes followed. A few campers took large gulps of their beverages to empty the cans. "Believe me, this is a good thing," Blake assured them. "We will be carrying our garbage with us, so the less bulk the better."

One of the girls scrunched up her nose. "We're carrying our garbage?" she asked.

"Yes," Blake responded matter-of-factly. "Leave no trace. Which also means that you are not allowed to disturb—and by "disturb" I mean "take," any pretty rocks or historical artifacts. Admire them, certainly, but leave them there. They are not souvenirs. And, I will be checking everyone's pockets for contraband." This comment produced more nervous laughter from the campers. "We have several meals to prepare and the evenings can get chilly, so we'll need a good fire," he continued. "There's plenty of firewood on the forest floor, and we'll all need to do our part to collect it. So, no matter how hungry or cold you are, you may not cut down any live vegetation. That includes trees, plants, and flowers." He scanned the group. His gaze stopped on Marta. He blinked. "…. to put in your hair."

Kirsten's head snapped toward Blake. She stood. "That's right," she said. "They'll be no beauty contests, so just leave nature's beauty alone."

Blake looked down at his notes. "I hope you all brought along a good wind-breaker, and if not, you can purchase one at the front desk." He awkwardly modeled the one he was wearing which triggered a chuckle from the group and all out laughter from Kirsten. "And finally, we don't have any bathrooms in the BWCA. No toilets, no biffies, no porta-potties. Most campsites have an open-air commode set back from the campsite which we'll need to share."

"Open air? Like no walls?" A young woman asked.

"That's right. No walls."

"We like to call it 'The Throne'," Kirsten chimed in.

"And if you need to go, and someone is already on the throne, find a spot at least 200 feet from the shore to do your business," Blake said.

The women squirmed in their seats.

Blake then taught them how to pack their Duluth packs, and use a paddle properly (which, Marta later learned, was more complicated than she expected). The rest, he told them, they would learn as they go.

The group had three canoes, with two paddlers and one rider in each. On that crisp spring day, they piled into their assigned canoes. One man and two women in each. Marta and another woman were assigned to Blake's canoe. Marta volunteered to take the bow and Blake steered from the stern. They left the shore and with each dip of the paddle, the cool wind blew across Marta's face taking all her anxiety with it. She was astonished at how she could see things so much more clearly here in the untainted wilderness without the smog of the city clouding her view.

Blake led the way and Kirsten brought up the rear for the first leg of their journey, only a five-mile trek. Perfect for the newbies. Just long enough to get some much-needed paddling practice, as well as a taste of what was in store in the days to come. They landed at their campsite, pulled up and secured the canoes, unloaded their gear and began to set up camp. Obviously, they still had quite a lot to learn and do like pitch tents, start a campfire, and most importantly, hang their food in a tree to make sure bears didn't invade their provisions.

On day two, they broke down camp and learned about portaging. The three men would each carry a canoe. Blake demonstrated how to grasp the middle sides, left arm across right, and hoist the canoes overhead with the center yoke landing on their shoulders. Kirsten distributed the packs among the women and helped them lift and secure each. Off they trudged, following the rough, overgrown woodland path, stepping over rocks and logs, climbing up hills, and slogging through wetlands to the water on the other side.

While several members of her citified group groused about the mosquitos, the heat, portaging, the open-air thrones, and the just plain hard work, Marta felt reborn. Marta reveled in paddling through the quiet waters, listening to the mournful call of the loon, and breathing in the fresh air. She'd hike off on the rock formations and find a quiet spot to herself. She was amazed to discover how noisy the quiet was if you really listen. Birds chirped, bugs buzzed, squirrels chattered, and leaves rustled in the wind. The brightness of the night sky entranced her. It was packed full of stars. Stars that were never visible through the glare of city lights.

On day three, Marta noticed her pack seemed heavier than the other camper's packs, and while unpacking her pack, she looked up to find Blake watching her.

"You carried all that?" Blake asked.

"Yep. Do I get a reward?" she responded proudly.

He just smiled.

On day four, Marta was sent off to collect firewood. She passed by Blake with her arms full as she returned to camp.

"You sure are industrious," Blake said.

"Kirsten says I need to carry my own weight around here. So, I'm doing my best."

"Let me help you. Might be a chilly night tonight."

They went back into the woods together.

"You've got a great job," Marta commented as she snapped a good-sized stick in half across her knee.

Blake bent down and picked up a pine branch. "Yeah, I sure did miss it the last two summers."

"Miss it?" she asked as she threw more sticks into her pile.

"I was a law clerk the last two summers. And this will be my last trip as a BWCA guide." He scratched his bristly chin. "I was a guide during my college years, but if you're offered a clerkship during law school, you take it. So, before starting my career as a lawyer, I wanted one last summer in the BWCA." He winked at her. "Really grateful for it." He found a downed birch, picked it up by the end and started to drag it toward the campsite.

"I can imagine. This is Heaven." She gathered her pile of sticks and followed. "Where will you be practicing law?"

"Minneapolis. I'll have to head back to the cities after this week."

"Well, you can always come back for a visit. I certainly plan to." She set her firewood by the fire pit.

"Yes." He smiled. "You should."

On day five, and as usual, Marta was slated last in line for a sun shower. She laid the plastic water-filled bag in a sunny spot to be sure it would be nice and warm when her turn arrived. She had come to love the sun shower experience. She found something invigorating about standing practically naked in the forest with the open water bag that was hanging from a branch above, pouring down over her and washing away the sweat and dust accumulated from the day's activities.

Marta watched as Kirsten went off, sun shower bag in hand, and then took a seat near the campfire waiting for her turn, with bio degradable shampoo in hand and towel ready.

Blake appeared, looking more like a mountain man with each passing day. "What are you waiting for?"

"My turn for a sun shower."

"You don't need a sun shower."

"Oh, indeed I do," she disagreed.

"Are you wearing your suit?"

"Yes," she answered hesitantly. He held out his hand. "Come with me." He led her to a large rock shelf that hung over the water. "There's plenty of fresh water here." He smiled at her, set his towel down and jumped in. He rose to the surface and flipped the bangs from his face, his scruffy, wet whiskers glistening in the sun. "Come on in," he called. "The water's fine."

She looked at him skeptically. She had felt the water, and it was not fine. It was cold.

"Come join me, Marta," he called out.

A tingle ran through her. She loved the way he said her name. *Why hadn't she noticed that before?* She stripped down to her swimming suit and leapt in after him, coming to the surface with a high-pitched scream.

He laughed. "You'll get used to it in a minute." "You're crazy!" She puffed. "It's freezing in here!"

"If it were freezing, it would be ice." He laughed. "We call this exhilarating." He dove under and scrubbed his scalp. "We can't use the soap in here, but you'll be clean just the same."

She followed suit. Surprisingly enough, she soon acclimated to the temperature and had to agree, exhilarating described it perfectly. Back on the shore they dried off.

"Why doesn't she like me?" Marta asked.

Blake looked at her. "You mean Kirsten."

"Yes."

"It's not that she doesn't like you," Blake said to the rock under their feet. "She's jealous."

"Jealous? What in the world does she have to be jealous about?"

Blake looked up at her coyly, "She sees the way I look at you."

Marta felt the flush fill her cheeks. After being in Crystal's shadow for so long, the idea seemed preposterous. Then she remembered what it was like to be discarded. "Are you two in a relationship?"

He shook his head. "No. I'm not interested in Kirsten. But I hear she has a crush on me." Blake picked up a rock from the shore and flung it across the water. They watched it skip, one, two, three, four, five times. His eyes looked south searching the shoreline for more rocks. "So, would you go out with me tonight?" he asked.

Out? Tonight? *Where in the world would they go on an island with a campsite full of campers?* She wondered.

"After dinner?" He picked up another rock and skipped it across the water.

Marta pointed at the skipping rock. "If you teach me how to do that, you have a date." She smiled.

"Deal," he agreed.

As Marta approached the tent, Kirsten arrived from the woods. "I heard screaming," she said. She noticed Marta's still wet head. "Did you fall in?"

"Believe it or not, I jumped in," Marta explained with a big smile on her face.

"You jumped in?"

"Yes," Marta said. They both turned as Blake came up from the shore, towel around his shoulders. "And it was exhilarating!"

Later that evening, Blake and Marta found a quiet, private spot away from the group. Blake pulled out a Hershey Bar he'd pilfered from the s'mores provisions. "This is the best I could do for dessert."

A Canada Jay landed on the branch in a nearby white pine. Blake pointed at the bird. "Watch out," he warned. "A camp robber is here."

"It's a bird," Marta said.

"Yes, but this is not just any bird," Blake told her. "This is a Gray Jay, well known to us campers for their boldness and thievery."

The Jay dropped down to the rock below and started hopping closer.

Marta laughed with delight.

"Hold on to your chocolate," Blake cautioned. "These birds are not shy."

The bird took a short flight and landed just to Marta's left startling her. She shrieked.

Blake stood to shoo it away and the wrapper fell out of his pocket.

Marta picked it up. "Leave no trace."

He took the wrapper from her hand. "Where have you been all my life?" He leaned down and kissed her.

One week under the stars was all it took. They had an instant connection.

On the last night of their trip, while she and Blake sat by the shore, she saw the glory of the northern lights flashing green and pink across the night sky.

◆ ◆ ◆

"Marta?" Blake said pulling her back from memory lane. She felt his warm embrace. *When had things changed?* she wondered. What was it Crystal had said that morning? The words whirled in her head: 'Don't try to stop me, I just can't keep it secret any longer.'

She stepped out of Blake's arms. "I told Matt about Crystal."

Chapter 16

"Y"ou lost him?" Petruco exclaimed.

"Yes," Red said. "I thought he just went to the bathroom."

Petruco clenched his jaw, the veins on his neck bulged. "You *thought* he went to the bathroom?"

Red shoved his hands into his pockets. "Yes, but it led to a shared hallway. He must have gone out through the door at the back."

"Why didn't you follow him?" Petruco threw up his hands.

Red shrugged and rattled off his reasons. "The door he went through was labeled 'Bathroom,' he left his coffee cup on the table, I had a seat by the coffee shop entrance, and I had a clear view of his car." He clenched his hands together and added sullenly, "I didn't expect the idiot would leave without his Jaguar."

Petruco tapped Red's forehead with his pointer finger. "Well it appears he's smarter than you think." He shook his head in disgust. "He probably knew you were tailing him."

Red stared at the floor, disgraced. He had lost him, but he didn't believe for one instant that Garrett knew he had been followed. In his years of surveillance, he learned people who suspect cops are following them are looking for someone hiding behind a corner or a bush, not someone right there in their face.

"And how many people own Jaguars?" Petruco asked. "Not many," he said, answering his own question. "So, if he didn't want to be followed, he knew he had to ditch the car." He pushed his pointer finger in Red's chest. "And you should have seen that coming a mile away."

"He didn't know I was following him," Red countered defensively.

"He *knew* and he shook you," Petruco said.

Isaac thought he saw tears well in Red's eyes. "Or somebody took him," Isaac offered.

Red turned and glared at Isaac. "Why didn't you arrest him when you had the chance? He was right there, ready and willing."

"Right," Vick agreed. "We should have arrested him."

Red stared at Vick again astounded that they were on the same side. Even more unbelievable, the same side opposite Isaac.

Petruco cocked his bird head at Isaac. "What's he talking about?"

"During his interview—" Isaac began.

"He said 'I suppose you're going to arrest me," Red interrupted, mimicking Garrett.

"He put his wrists on the table just waiting for the cuffs," Vick added.

Red shook his head and looked at Isaac. "I told you then I thought you should have arrested him, didn't I?"

Isaac turned toward Petruco. "We didn't have enough solid evidence. We arranged to get search warrants for his home and gym."

Petrucco's eyes narrowed. "But now he's gone."

"We had plenty of evidence," Vick said, countering Isaac's statement. "Garrett was the last known person to see her alive, he admits they argued, she was shot with his gun and he obviously wanted her money." He turned toward Isaac and held up his palms toward the sky. "What more do you need?"

"Dude is crazy, man," Red said.

Isaac took a deep breath and kept focused on Petruco. He knew it wasn't the time to get into a row with his partners. "I don't think he did it. I'm not saying he didn't have anything to do with it," he said. "I just thought we'd learn more by following him. He's scared of something."

"I think your spidey sense left you on this one, partner," Vick declared.

Petruco's vulture-like eyes settled on Isaac. Past experience had taught him not to discount him. Isaac had proven, time-tested, accurate instincts.

"Somethings going on with him," Isaac continued. "He wanted to be arrested. And nobody wants to be arrested unless a jail cell offers protection. I thought we'd learn more by following him."

"But now he's gone," Petruco repeated and threw his hands up in exasperation. How on earth was he going to play this with the media? Worse yet, how would he explain this to the mayor?

"Yes," Isaac said.

Petruco's beady eyes looked them all up and down. "Get that search warrant. Impound his car. Find him!" Petruco then stormed off head first, his feet doing their best to keep up.

Isaac looked at Vick and Red, disheartened and incensed at the same time. "You heard him. Get that search warrant. Impound his car."

◆ ◆ ◆

They all gathered at the table, and after their dinner prayer, opened the bucket of chicken and dug in.

"How was your day, kids?" Isaac hoped that their day had been much better than his.

Jacob grinned. "I saw Avery with John Rogers today."

Avery turned bright red. "So?"

Jacob raised his brows. "So, what does Jessica think of that?"

"How would I know?" Avery retorted.

Isaac looked back and forth between the two of them. "Who is John Rogers?" He was much more concerned with his daughter's interest in a young man than what whoever Jessica was thought about it.

"He's the center on the basketball team," Jacob told him. Then he turned and made little kissy noises at Avery.

"Stop it!" Avery snapped.

"Okay, that's enough kids." Claudia gave Isaac a look that said she'd fill him in later.

"He's really tall," Isabelle added.

Avery let out a screech of exasperation.

"Well, I had an incredible day," Claudia said, changing the subject. "I can't wait for you all to come see my new office."

Dinner done, the kids scattered to their own rooms to tackle homework.

Isaac and Claudia carried the leftovers to the counter. Walter sat between the table and the counter, ready to snatch up any scraps that may fall to the floor.

"What's going on with Avery?" Isaac asked. Claudia wiped her hands on a kitchen towel. "It seems that we have a love triangle. This boy John is paying attention to Avery, even though by all reports, he's dating a girl named Jessica."

"I hate him already," Isaac said. "Isn't she too young to care about boys?"

Claudia rolled her eyes. "She's in seventh grade, Isaac. That's *all* girls in seventh grade think about."

Isaac handed Claudia the milk glasses across the counter. Walter's eyes followed his every movement. "Well, I'll certainly have a talk with her about that," he said. "I don't care *how* tall he is."

"You'll do nothing of the sort," Claudia said. "They'll figure it out." She opened up the dishwasher door.

Isaac picked up the plates from the table accidently stepping on Walter's tail. Walter yelped.

"Out of the way, dog."

Claudia cocked her head at him.

He set the plates on the counter. "She'll get her heart broken."

Claudia leaned across the counter and took his face in her hands. "She might." She gave him a peck on the lips. "But isn't that part of the learning process?" She released him and set her hands firmly on the countertop. "Forbidding this will just make her want it more," she warned. "She needs to learn to recognize a cad. It might hurt for a while, but it will be in her best interest in the long run." Her eyes searched his face. He'd been quieter than usual all evening.

He looked away. "I don't like it."

"We can't shield her from everything. She's going to have to take a few lumps. We'll just always be there to support her." She moved around the counter and took him in her arms. "You're a bit on edge tonight. How did *your* day go?"

He sat at the table. Walter trod over and lay his head on Isaacs lap. Isaac scratched behind Walter's ears. "Not great," he confessed.

Claudia raised her brows in concern. Her stoic husband didn't often admit to experiencing distress.

"Remember that client's husband you warned me about?" he asked.

"Yes. I was worried about you." She joined him at the table. "What happened?"

"He came in for an interview today. I could have arrested him, but I let him go." He sighed deeply. "Then he shook the tail."

"Oh." She took his hand and they sat in silence for a few minutes.

"They threw me under the bus," he said.

"Who threw you under the bus?"

"Vick and Red. They said it was my fault. That I should have arrested him."

"I can see Vick doing that, but Red too?"

"He was under the gun. He's the one who lost him."

◆ ◆ ◆

The search of Garrett's car yielded few clues, in fact it was quite clean. They found the usual stuff in the glove compartment, an owner's manual, tissues, a window scrapper, a tire gauge, and a pack of gum. No bag of bloody clothes, no threatening notes, no divorce papers, and no cell phone. The luminol spray revealed no blood stains on the surface. They would now take the car apart to check under the upholstery for hidden stains in case the surface area had been recently cleaned. If there was blood, they would find it.

Garrett had not returned home, but they'd watch the house through the night. Tomorrow, they would search it.

Chapter 17

Glory be – it's Marta!" exclaimed Edna. She always greeted Marta that way. "Aren't you a sight for sore eyes!" She lowered the footrest and sat upright in her recliner. "What brings you 'round this way?"

"Oh Edna, you dear, I wanted to see how you're doing. I brought you some flowers and soup," Marta said, adding, "It's the cure for whatever ails you." She set the vase on the end table next to Edna. "I'll just put the soup in the refrigerator."

"What a gem you are!" Edna hollered toward the kitchen. "You know, the doctors, they won't let me do hardly anything. Poor Gib has to take care of me. Not what he's used to, you know. Not what I'm used to either. Feels off, and I don't like it one bit. I much prefer to be the caretaker."

"Oh, I know you do, Edna," Marta said as she returned from the kitchen. "You take good care of everyone, but now it's time for us to take care of you for a change." She noticed the bandaged area on Edna's head. "Now let me take a look at that." Edna leaned forward. The doctors had shaved the area all around the wound leaving a circle of Edna's wispy gray hair hanging in a horseshoe shape around it. If she had red hair, she would have looked a bit like a clown wearing a little white cap. Marta bent down and gave Edna a gentle squeeze. "Oh Edna, I'm so sorry!"

"I'm fine. Don't you worry 'bout me."

Marta sat on the couch.

"Edna reached up and gently felt the area around the wound. "Still smarts a bit, but the doctor says I'll heal up just fine. She looked at Marta with raised brows, "Twelve stitches!" she bragged. "I hear old skin tears easily."

Marta's head dropped. "Twelve stitches. You poor thing!"

"Oh now, I know you've got other things weighing on you." She reached over and patted Marta's hand. "I know you're hurting, honey. We'll both surely miss Crystal, but you especially." They sat in silence for a moment. "Can't imagine what could have happened." She shook her head. "I didn't hear the news that she had passed until after they patched me up in the hospital and a policeman sat by my bed." She looked at Marta. "Do you know he asked me if I thought Crystal would take her own life? Can you imagine? I told him no, of course. In fact, I told him she'd been happier lately than I've ever seen her. Isn't that right? I know you saw it too."

Marta nodded.

"Finally getting rid of that no-good husband, you know. That's a load off."

"Yes, indeed. Getting rid of Garrett finally," Marta concurred. "She'd talked about it for years. I wonder what made her finally take the step."

Edna leaned forward. "Love," she said with a twinkle in her eye. "I think she'd found a beau."

Marta shifted in her seat. "If she did, she didn't mention it to me."

"Nor me neither, but I figured she just didn't want to share that news 'til the divorce was done."

"Right. Right," Marta said. "That's probably it."

"Makes this all the more tragic." They sat in silence considering this for a moment. "You know, they wanted to know everything I did that day from the time I crawled out of bed," Edna continued. "But I don't see how that has anything to do with it. 'Lest they think I killed her. But I told them, one minute I was starting in on work and the next I come to in the hallway."

"So, you didn't see anyone in the house?"

"Nope. Not a sole."

"Good," Marta said. "I mean, I'm glad you didn't get in the middle of something. That could have been much worse."

"If I'd been there, maybe none of this would have happened." Tears welled in Edna's blue eyes. "Poor, poor Crystal, God rest her soul. She didn't deserve to die so young."

"No." Marta took Edna's hand in hers. "But she will be with us always in our memories."

Edna smiled at that. "Indeed she will."

The bedroom door opened and Gib stuck his head in the room. "Ma, it's time to get ready."

"Look!" Edna said. "Marta stopped by to check in on me."

"Hey," Gib grunted with a wave of his hand and then left down the hallway.

"Hi Gib," Marta called after him, and then turned toward Edna. "You need to get ready?"

Edna nodded. "That nice detective is coming to take me back to the house today to look around. First thing I'm going to do is tell him about them boots."

"Boots?" Marta asked.

"Yep," Edna confirmed. "When I came in that day I saw Crystal's car in the garage so I knew she was home and I thought Garrett was there because there were men's boots at the front door. But you know, it didn't strike me 'til later that I hadn't seen Garrett's car." She leaned in. "So, I think those boots belonged to the killer."

"Really." Marta shifted in her seat. "What do you remember about the boots? I mean, was there anything distinctive about them?"

"Oh yes. They were those Steger boots. I know 'cause my Earl had a pair just like 'em. They're expensive, you know, that's why I assumed they belonged to Garrett." She shook her head. "You know Garrett, always spending money on something."

"Yes. Right," Marta agreed. "Always spending money," she repeated. "So you're sure you didn't maybe miss seeing Garrett's car? Maybe he parked on the street somewhere?"

"Nope. Didn't see it anywhere."

Marta stood. "Well, I'd better get going and let you get ready for your appointment. I'll stop back tomorrow and you can tell me all about it."

Edna clapped her hands together. "I'd love it!"

Marta bent down and gave Edna a hug. She looked into Edna's clear blue eyes, "I'm so sorry, Edna."

"Thank you dear. Your visit has lifted my spirits. We'll get through this together, won't we?"

Marta nodded, pulled on her coat, and headed toward the door. She stopped in the doorway and her head dropped to her chest. "Edna," she said.

"Yes dear?"

She turned to face her. "I have a confession to make."

"Yes, dear?"

She sighed. "Patty made the soup."

Edna smiled. "Well, whoever made it, it was sure nice of you to think of me."

"She brought it to me because Matt has been sick," she explained.

"And she wanted to gossip," Edna added.

Marta smiled. "Yes, first and foremost that, I imagine."

"Then I won't be mentioning anything to her about where that soup ended up. You can count on me to keep your confidences anytime, dear."

"Thanks, Edna. I'd appreciate that. Hope you enjoy it. You know she really is a good cook."

Chapter 18

They descended on the townhouse like a swarm of bees, ready to take it apart inch by inch. Isaac stepped up to the door, warrant in hand. A crisp breeze blew across his face. He knocked. No response.

The garage door to the townhouse next door opened and a brown Toyota Corolla backed out. The driver stopped the car midway down the driveway and got out. "What's going on here?" he called out.

With a jerk of his head, Isaac directed an officer to engage him.

The officer crossed through the snow toward the neighbor. "Have you seen anyone coming or going from this house recently?"

"No," the neighbor responded. "We're on different schedules. I don't think he works."

Isaac knocked again a bit louder and rang the doorbell. He could hear the buzz of the doorbell inside, but there was no sign of life.

"I hear him coming home late at night most nights," the neighbor added.

"Did you hear him coming home last night?" the officer asked.

"No, but I noticed that car sat here all night." He pointed at the surveillance vehicle.

The officer nodded.

Isaac knocked and rang one more time. Silence.

"What did he do?" the neighbor asked.

"We're just trying to locate him," the officer said.

The neighbor scanned the throng of police officers and vehicles. "Sure," he said.

"Have a nice day." The officer crossed back through the snow.

Isaac stepped aside to let the tactical team get the door open. A few minutes later they were inside. Although still unkempt, the place had been picked up since Isaac's last visit. A single light shone from above the stove, but otherwise all was dark. "Mr. Holt?" Isaac called out. No answer. "Mr. Holt?" he called again.

One by one the tactical team entered and spread out to their assigned spots while another team began the search of the outside area surrounding the home. Inside, drawers and closets would be emptied checking each article inside and then the container itself for items that may be taped on the back or underside or in hidden compartments. Cupboards would be unpacked, furniture would be checked, picture frames would be removed from the walls and examined, and everything would be dusted for fingerprints. No article of clothing, no carpet fiber, no strand of hair would go uncollected. Outside, the exterior of the home would be searched, footprints in the snow would be molded, and the trash would be inspected. Nothing would be overlooked.

Isaac sniffed the air. His nose led him to the trash container under the sink full of smashed beer cans. He opened up the refrigerator. More beer, your basic condiments in the door, and a couple Styrofoam containers of leftovers from the casino. He opened up the freezer. Empty. He opened up the cupboards. Practically barren. He strolled through the rest of the home, finding only the essentials—an unmade bed, a desk, a large screen television, somewhere to sit. No adornments whatsoever.

Garrett did not plan on staying here long, thought Isaac.

And Isaac couldn't stay any longer either. He needed to move on to his next appointment. It would be a busy day. He would let the experts finish their work. For Red's sake, and his own, he hoped they would find something to help them locate Garrett and break this case open.

He stepped out into the cold air. As usual, it hadn't taken long for the reporters to find out about the search and show up with their cameras rolling and microphones in hand. They lunged at him as he made his way to his car, peppering him with questions. "Isn't this the house of

Crystal Holt's husband?" "Is Garrett Holt suspected of killing his wife?" "Do you have him in custody?" "What was the motive?" "Will there be a trial?"

To all their interrogatories Isaac said, "No comment."

The neighbors caught wind as well. All along the townhouse development cars sat in their driveways keeping the occupants warm while they watched the scene unfold. The running vehicles' exhaust created an eerie fog over the area.

Isaac opened his car door and took a seat. Two reporters moved inside his opened door blocking his ability to close it without injuring them. "I have no comment," he repeated. "Please move aside."

Then, like a crowd following a long pass at a football game, all their heads turned as they watched the Lincoln Town Car arrive on the scene. Within seconds, they sprinted down the road, practically tackling each other, to be the first to get the scoop.

Isaac breathed a sigh of relief as he closed the door and started his engine. He pressed the button to heat the seat, turned up the defroster, and watched as Petruco emerged from the Town Car and allowed the press to gather around. He looked dapper and confident as he held up his gloved hands to silence the group. Isaac had to admit Petruco had a certain charisma with the public. No doubt Petruco felt the pressure to solve this crime, and the captain wanted to be the hero. Isaac shook his head. He fervently hoped Petruco didn't say anything he'd have to retract later, because if he did, there was sure to be a scapegoat.

Chapter 19

It was turning into a beautiful sunny day. All the snow of the previous two days had been expertly cleared from the roads.

Isaac pulled the cat carrier from the back seat, headed up the walkway to the little white house with green trim, and knocked on the door.

Gib opened the door and looked him up and down.

"Gib, I'm Detective Scott and I'm here…" Gib held up his hand and stopped Isaac mid-sentence with that don't waste my time look young often assume when an adult prattles on with pleasantries. "I remember who you are and I know why you're here," he said. He stood aside, flipped his head, and invited Isaac in.

Isaac stepped inside and set the cat carrier down in the entryway. Edna's voice called out from the living room. "Yoo, hoo! Hello detective! I knew I put my trust in the right man," she said. She joyfully clasped her hands together. "It's so nice to have Ebony home!"

"My pleasure, Edna," Isaac said. "Although the cat didn't care much for the ride."

Edna laughed. "Oh, that's the honest truth! Ebony hates car rides."

Isaac realized she was familiar with the unearthly noises that came out of the cat while traveling in a car.

"I believe he soiled himself."

Another laugh. "Always did. Crystal scheduled vet appointments for days I would be there so I could clean him up." She winked at him. "She wasn't blessed with the nurturing gene I am so it suited me just fine." She turned her attention to Gib. "Gib, get Eb cleaned up, please."

Gib picked up the cat carrier. "Come on, cat," he said and headed toward the kitchen in the back of the house.

As Isaac removed his coat, he watched Gib gently pull the cat from the carrier and set him in the sink, all Gib's earlier gruffness gone. Gib wet some paper towels and delicately wiped the cat's underside. Isaac could almost hear Ebony's purr as he rubbed his cheek against Gib's face. Gib returned the gesture with affection. Isaac stepped out of his shoes and entered the living room. "How are you feeling today, Edna?"

"Oh, I'm coming along like a stage coach across the plains. Kinda bumpy, but making headway." She smiled.

Gib entered the room with Ebony wrapped in a blanket and set him on Edna's lap. "She'd be doing much better if you'd arrest that cheater." His surliness had returned. "Why haven't you arrested him yet?" He didn't wait for an answer and stomped back to the kitchen.

"Cheater?" Isaac asked.

Edna shook her head. "Gib's sore because Garrett hired him to do some kind of computer project and then never paid him for it. It doesn't have a thing to do with Crystal's murder."

"You know I can hear you, Mom," Gib said from the kitchen.

"Just like Garrett, I suppose," she continued. "I told Gib this is one of those hard life lessons." She turned her head toward the kitchen entrance. Loudly, she added, "Sometimes it's hard to know who to trust."

Gib stomped back into the room. He looked directly at Isaac. "We had a contract. Fifteen hundred dollars—a total bargain for the work I did. Then he had the nerve to say the program didn't work! It works—it works great!" He shook his head. "The idiot just didn't enter the data correctly. Just plain user error. Not my fault. I spent hours developing the program and even more hours trying to train him how to use it." He shook his head. "What a dope. He couldn't even figure out how to get his stuff saved to the Cloud. A total idiot," he declared and left the room again.

Edna turned toward Isaac. "Oh, he may look like a stray dog and snarl like one too, but he's smart."

"I can still hear you, Mom," Gib called.

"He's a genius, they tell me. Got a full scholarship to MIT," she continued. "Starts in the fall."

"You must be very proud," Isaac said.

"Couldn't be more so." She smiled and turned her head toward the kitchen. "Go get ready for work now, Gib." She caught Isaac's eye, held her finger to her mouth and listened for the bedroom door to close. "You know the boy's had a tough life," she explained. "When he came here to live with us, he had a lot of demons to deal with." She reached over and pat Isaac on the knee. "But deal with them we did. Head on. You know, I couldn't be more proud of my Gibson if he had been my own biological child."

Gib resurfaced without the hoodie, his white shirt showing the Geek Squad logo. He draped the narrow black tie around his neck. "I'm off now, Mom." He bent down and gave her a tender kiss on the head. He held her shoulders. "Now don't overdo today. You know what the doctors said." He turned and looked at Isaac sternly. "Take care of her. She really shouldn't go out today— and you should get Garrett behind bars where he belongs."

"Gib, don't badger the man," she scolded.

"Ha!" He opened the door and looked back at Isaac. "He better hope that YOU get him before somebody else does."

Isaac watched Gib drive off in an old Chevy Cavalier while Edna pulled her coat from the entryway closet.

"Allow me." He took hold of the collar allowing Edna to place her arms easily into the sleeves.

"A gentleman," she declared. "Your momma raised you right."

He smiled at her, taking particular notice of the top of her head. "Edna, are you sure you're up to this today?"

"You know those doctors tell me not to do hardly anything. But they don't know I'm stubborn as an old goat and spry as a kid." She winked at Isaac. "Wild horses couldn't keep me away. I only pray I can be of some help. I already told that nice officer all I can remember." She raised her brows. "Although that wasn't much since I was knocked out cold." She smiled at Isaac. "You're smart to have me come take a look. I know that house better 'n anyone."

♦ ♦ ♦

They turned left onto Willow Lane. Marta's car was just pulling into her garage. "There's Marta!" Edna said. She looked at Isaac. "She brought me soup today." She grinned as if she had received a Congressional Medal of Honor.

"Oooh," Isaac said, hoping he sounded sufficiently impressed.

"That Marta," she went on. "She was Crystal's anchor. Always keeping her level. Bringing her back down to earth. Crystal had a habit of poking sleeping bears, you know."

He didn't know, but he nodded and wondered which bear Crystal had poked two days ago.

They parked on the street outside the yellow tape and donned their plastic gloves. Isaac helped Edna to the door.

She stood at the threshold. "Reckon this will be the last time I enter this house." She took a breath and stepped inside. She pointed to the entryway corner. "That's where the boots were."

Edna had reported seeing men's boots in the entryway the day of the murder. "Can you describe them for me, Edna?"

"Oh sure, they were Steger boots. My Earl had a pair. I figured they were Garrett's—just like him to go out and buy fancy new boots, you know. But now I don't think so 'cause his car wasn't here. He didn't go anywhere without that car, you know."

Interesting statement considering that's just what he did yesterday. "So, you hadn't ever seen those boots before?" Isaac asked.

"Nope. New boots."

"But now you don't think they were Garrett's."

"Not lest he walked here."

Or took a cab or uber, Isaac thought to himself. And there would be a record of that. "Men's boots?" Isaac asked to confirm.

"Men's boots," she confirmed.

They had collected several shoe and boot prints both at Crystal's home and Garrett's townhome. Size, tread, and markings would be studied and compared. Isaac recalled Garrett wearing Air Jordan's during their two interactions.

Edna walked up the half flight of stairs and started down the hallway. She pointed at the rust colored stain on the carpet. "That's where I fell."

"After you were hit."

"Yes," she said. "They tell me I was wacked with a skillet. Imagine that. A skillet. Everything went black. They tell me 'twas the cold air that made me come to."

"The cold air from the open front door."

"Yes. Must have left it open when he ran out."

"So you're sure it wasn't open before you were struck?"

Edna gave him a look. "Well, I certainly would have noticed that, now wouldn't I?"

Isaac nodded. "You certainly would have. So Edna, Would you please close your eyes and try to remember that day? Other than the boots, was there anything else amiss? -Smells? -Sounds?"

Edna took his arm and closed her eyes as he requested. "I pulled into the driveway. Got out and punched the garage door code."

"Did you notice any footprints on the driveway?"

She shook her head. "No, not that I recall," she said. "I went in through the garage door, hung up my coat, took off my boots and headed upstairs—just like always. I smelled coffee. Then whop!" She opened her eyes and looked at him. "Next thing I remember is waking up on the floor."

Oh well, Isaac thought to himself. "Take a look around, Edna, and let me know if anything is missing, out of place, changed, new or just different."

Edna walked through the house with Isaac following, noting her comments. She opened the kitchen cupboard. "Garrett's cup is missing," she told him. She walked into the dining room. "What's all this?" she asked. "Can I look?" Isaac nodded.

She picked up the manila envelope with the note from Marta and peered into the opening. "Looks like Crystal was decorating again. Not surprising, with the way she was jazzing everything up."

"Jazzing everything up?"

"Yep. She used to have me come once a week, but Crystal wanted me to start coming more often. Really wanted to spiff up the place. Had me even cleaning out closets and drawers. Really digging in. I liked it, you know. Usually people don't want you rummaging around through their stuff so I didn't do that kind of work 'lest asked to."

"Do you know why?"

"She never said, but I think she was just starting fresh. With everything. Out with the old, in with the new. Got rid of Garrett, throwing away all the useless things to free her soul," she paused, searching for the word. "What do they call that?"

"Cathartic?"

"Exactly. I knew you'd understand." She shook her head with a look of amazement. "You're a prize, aren't you. The way you listen. People like that, you know, when you really listen." She picked up the ring box from inside the basket with the Valentine banner and opened it. "Never seen this before."

"Any thoughts?"

She raised her brow. "The new beau? Garrett trying to woo her back? An impulse buy for herself?" She looked at Isaac. "She'd do that, you know. She loved her jewelry."

They moved down the hallway and into the bedroom. Edna gasped. A chalk outline showing Crystal's fate remained.

"Come pray with me," she said. Isaac moved in next to her. "Take my hand." And so he did, her hand so tiny inside his. They bowed their heads together.

"Heavenly Father," Edna began. "Though we may never understand why Crystal was tragically taken from us, bless this fine detective as he works to bring justice and closure for us all. Heavenly Father, while Crystal wasn't a regular church-goer, she had a good heart and never meant to hurt anyone. Please wrap her in your loving arms and show her that unconditional, everlasting love she was so desperate to find. We here on earth have peace knowing she is in your care. In Jesus' name, Amen." She looked at Isaac and patted his hand. "You have strong hands, detective. I can feel the Holy Spirit running right through you."

"Edna, that's the nicest thing anyone's ever said to me." He smiled at her. "And I certainly appreciate the prayers."

She looked around the room and the bathroom and confirmed that Crystal would not have left her jewelry strewn all over the dresser. Otherwise, things were in place. She also didn't see that any particular piece of jewelry was missing.

"I don't know what else to tell you, detective. But if anyone knows the neighborhood scuttlebutt, it's Patty."

"Patty?"

She walked him to the front window and pointed across the street. "Patty lives right there. She and her binoculars know what everyone on Willow Lane is up to."

"Binoculars?" he asked.

She smiled. "Yes, binoculars. She keeps them right by the front picture window." She leaned toward him as if she had something juicy to share. "Why, I remember one day I come upstairs and found Crystal parading around in her birthday suit. Can you imagine? And she says to me, 'Peeking Patty is at it again, so I thought I'd give her a show.'" She looked at Isaac with her twinkling blue eyes. "Then she says, 'C'mon Edna, why don't you join me?' and before I could say a word, Crystal shimmied right there in front of the picture window. Lord forgive me, I must admit that I laughed out loud." Then she added gleefully, "It was delightfully scandalous!"

Isaac thought she suddenly looked like a mischievous little school girl.

"Then Crystal said, 'That should give Patty something new to gossip about.'" Edna shook her head. "You know, Patty spends so much time examining everyone else's life, I don't know how she has enough time for her own." She shrugged. "But maybe it's not much of a life."

Isaac remembered Vick had interviewed most of the neighbors and didn't have much to report. "I'll be sure to speak with her," he assured Edna.

"If you do, don't let her veer off," she warned. "She's a water bug, that one."

Isaac crinkled his brow.

"Always zig-zagging around. Can't keep to a straight line," she explained.

"Thanks for the warning," Isaac said. "I think we can wrap it up here. Let me get your coat."

He took the coat from the coat rack and held it open for her. She slid her arms inside. "Edna, I have to ask," he said. "Do you think Garrett could have done this?"

She shook her head, "I just don't know—'specially since his car weren't here." She thought about it for a long minute, then grabbed his forearm. "But, I'm going to leave the detecting up to you, detective. 'Cause I can see how smart you are. I see it in your eyes."

Before stepping outside, Edna took one last look around. "I surely miss Crystal and all her nonsense. She was like family. And I've grown quite fond of this place. It feels a bit like losing my own home, I've cared for it for so long."

Realizing that she was now out of a job, Isaac started to wonder about her financial situation. He took her arm and escorted her to the car. "Edna what are your plans going forward? Will you need to find work?"

"Oh, money's no worry," she told him. "Earl's pension is fine." She looked into Isaac's face. "But life ain't nothin' lest you got people to care for."

"You've got Gib."

"I do. I do have Gib," she agreed. "But he'll be leaving me soon."

Isaac nodded remembering the full scholarship to MIT.

"I'll just ask God for someone to care for," she said. "God will provide."

Chapter 20

S he opened the door before he could knock.

"Ms. Olson?" he asked.

"*Mrs.* Olson," she corrected.

"Mrs. Olson, I'm Detective Scott of the Minneapolis Police Department."

"Oh yes," she interrupted. "I recognize you. You were here the day Crystal was murdered."

"Yes, that's correct. Mrs. Olson, may I have a few minutes of your time?"

"It's Patty, actually. Call me Patty," she said with a flip of her wrist. "All my friends do." She smiled and waited for him to try it again.

"May I have a few minutes of your time, Patty?"

"Of course, detective. Please come in." She stood aside and made a wide sweeping gesture with her arm to welcome him in. He stepped inside the massive, two-story entryway. "Let me take your coat." It was an offer that sounded more like an order. "Oh, and please remove your shoes—we mustn't bring in all that nasty slush."

Isaac dutifully removed his shoes and placed them on the rug next to the doorway. She took his coat and hung it in the entryway closet. The formal living room stood to the left of the entry. A large picture window offered a perfect view of the Holt's house directly across the street. He scanned the room and took particular notice of the set of binoculars sitting on the end table in front of the picture window just where Edna said they would be.

"I suspected you might have more questions for me." She flipped her hair over her shoulder. "The officer who stopped by that afternoon seemed a bit…" she paused and pursed her lips. "How do I put this delicately?" Isaac waited, curious to hear how she would describe Vick. "Dull," she pronounced. She raised her perfectly plucked brows and increased her pitch. "I gave him some very valuable information and he barely wrote anything down. I hope this interview produces some results." She shook her head. "I can't imagine why you haven't arrested Garrett yet." She shook her pointer finger in his direction, the bangles around her wrist jingling. "That fiend is bound to skip town. Better nab him quick." She turned abruptly, her blond hair flying to her back. "Come. Follow me."

She led him toward the back of the house into the spacious family room. She paused deliberately to admire the south wall. His eyes followed her gaze. She smiled. "I see you're admiring the artwork," she said proudly. "You won't believe this when I tell you, but I painted them all."

He was indeed surprised. He would have guessed that one of her children had painted them. More than twenty rectangular, stretched-canvas paintings covered the wall. The subject matter included various flower arrangements, lake scenes, mountain scenes, and fruit bowls. "It appears you have a passion for painting," he commented.

"I do. I find it so freeing! With my very busy life I need a creative release. *So* many people depend on me." She drew out the word 'so' to make it clear that there truly were a lot. "It's nice to do something that is all for me." She brought her hands to her cheeks. "Oh, but don't misunderstand me, detective. I'd hate for you to think I'm selfish, because I am certainly not. I would never neglect those that need me." She gazed lovingly at her paintings. "But, my Howard is always encouraging my extracurricular activities. He knows how imaginative I am. He says 'Paint! Paint! Paint!' He LOVES my work." She smiled at Isaac. "I can't blame him. They really are beautiful, don't you think?" She didn't wait for a reply and Isaac stifled a sigh of relief. "And that's not bragging, you understand. When it's the truth there's really no point in denying it. I go to *Art 4 All* to do all my work. That's where all my friends and I can paint together. Our instructor, John, has been getting a bit snippy lately, though." She raised her eyebrows. "I think he's having some problems with his boyfriend." She added under her breath, "You know how *they* can be."

"They?" thought Isaac. Edna's words ran through his head. Don't let her veer off. Sage advice. He remembered how concerned Patty was about the notes Vick didn't take at the last interview, so he pulled out his notepad. "So that information that you were giving the officer that stopped by," he said changing the subject. "What can you tell me about that?"

Her mouth snapped shut and she turned to face him. "Ah, let me tell you. Well first off, that Garrett Holt is a Neanderthal. Crystal wanted so badly to befriend us, but my Howard didn't want to associate with that caveman." Patty paused and eyed the notepad.

"Caveman." Isaac wrote.

She smiled. "He would just sit on the deck and shoot at birds and squirrels."

"Shoot?"

"BBs."

"Ah."

"He hit them quite often too."

"And you know this because?"

"Well when you hear that kind of ruckus you have to check it out," she said. "I would have called the police, but I didn't want to embarrass Crystal." She looked at Isaac and then at his note pad.

Isaac wrote "Shoots at birds and squirrels."

"And that proves it. He's absolutely capable of shooting to kill." She pointed at the note pad, "Get that down."

Isaac wrote "Shoots to kill."

"My Howard totally agrees. He can't believe you haven't arrested Garrett yet either. I was so relieved when they split. We couldn't wait to get Garrett out of the neighborhood." She raised her eyebrows again, which Isaac now realized indicated she was about to say something he was expected to write down. "But that brings me to the motive. We better sit down for this."

She sat on the white leather couch and Isaac took the chair to the side. A large photo of Patty and a man who must have been Howard sat on the table between them. It was the kind of portrait photo one has taken in a studio where you are posed just so and told when to smile. The couple looked like they could have been department store mannequins, which is exactly the look Isaac imagined Patty was going for.

Isaac held the notepad front and center, his pen poised and ready for more note taking.

"Crystal was having an affair," she declared. She paused for effect. She raised her eyebrows. "With someone right here on Willow Lane." Her eyebrows shifted even higher. "Her best friend's husband no less."

Isaac began to write "Affair with…" and looked to Patty to fill in the blank.

"Blake Coburn. His wife, Marta, is Crystal's best friend." She shook her head. "Shameful. Just shameful."

"Why do you think they were having an affair, Patty?"

She smiled. She obviously liked hearing her name. "Oh detective, EVERYONE thought so." She rolled her eyes. "Blake and Crystal showed up to the school hockey games and sat together way up in the rafters."

"Hockey." Isaac wrote.

"I'm not here to judge, you understand. And I don't gossip. I'm just telling you the facts. I know very well that none of us is perfect, detective. Even me! Honestly, that's why I go to confession every day. Well, I used to go every day until Father John told me I should only come once a month so he could free up his time for other souls in true need of forgiveness. He's such a saint."

She had veered off again. His ears started to hurt. "Tell me more about the hockey games," Isaac said.

"They sat up there and whispered together." She shook her head with distain. "It was just like Crystal to have an affair right out in the open. Always flaunting her beauty like some celebrity. You know she would walk around her house naked?"

It was Isaac's turn to raise his brows. *How much time did she spend with those binoculars?* Patty realized she may have said too much and defensively stuttered, "Well— well they never shut their curtains! Anyone could see right in."

In his line of work, nosy neighbors were often the key to solving crimes. She could be helpful if properly directed.

"Poor Marta," she said changing the focus of the conversation. "She didn't have a clue. Now, how can that be?"

"Other than the hockey games, were there any other signs of an affair between the two?"

She grinned like the Cheshire Cat. "I saw them buy jewelry together," she declared as if the final nail had been pounded in.

"Jewelry." Isaac wrote. "Can you tell me more about this?" "Oh yes. It was just last Saturday at the Minneapolis Mall. Kingston Jewelers."

"Saturday. Kingston Jewelers." Isaac wrote. *How did she know this?* "Where you in the store too?"

"I was in the mall, but saw them together in the store. Crystal was trying on rings!"

"Rings?"

"Yes. Rings." She nodded as if they were sharing a secret. "Crystal tried them all on and Blake waited patiently while she did. Considering how much time she spent lately watching the Home Shopping Network, I was a bit surprised she hadn't just ordered something already."

"Can you tell me approximately what time you saw them there?"

Patty shared the event details and Isaac dutifully filled his notebook.

"One final question, Patty. Do you think Garrett was aware of the affair?"

"Garrett? Not before that day, I don't. Honestly, I don't think Garrett is aware of much of anything." She shook her head. "He's been living elsewhere for the last three months. He just shows up on Tuesday mornings at 9:00 a.m. so they can go together to their counseling sessions. Which is probably why he was there that day. Normally, I would have been home, but I had a fundraising event.

My Howard was home in the morning, but had to catch a flight to Milwaukee, so he was gone by the time Garrett arrived. Too bad. We'd sure like to see him pay for what he did. As Howard says, Garrett's just a big bulldozer. No brains. No feelings. Destroys everything in his path."

Chapter 21

Isaac greeted them as they wiped the ink from their fingertips.

"Why were we fingerprinted?" Blake asked.

Marta felt her heart racing. *Yes, why?* Her prints were all over that house.

"Standard procedure," Isaac said. "So, we can identify which prints at the scene we can't identify."

Blake nodded, satisfied with the explanation.

"Thank you both for coming in," Isaac continued. "This is my colleague, Detective Marchese." Vick reached out to shake both of their hands. "He will be interviewing Mrs. Coburn."

"Excuse me, detective," Blake said. "But I thought we were here to give you insight on Crystal."

"Yes, that's true."

"Well. We can certainly do that better together, than if we are separated." He looked at his wife. "Don't you agree, Marta?"

"Yes." She nodded. "Yes. Together."

Isaac and Vick exchanged a glance. Considering the charge of adultery made by their neighbor, Isaac thought it best to separate the Coburns to try to get more honest, open answers.

"In fact, I insist we be interviewed together," Blake said. As a skilled attorney he knew it was never a good idea to talk to an officer without counsel present.

Isaac was surprised. He expected Blake would have welcomed this option to avoid the possibility of his affair being exposed to his wife. But, whether the Coburns were together or apart, it wouldn't change the way Isaac planned to conduct the interview— including questions regarding Blake's fidelity.

"That's fine," Isaac agreed and led them into the conference room at the end of the hall. As they took their seats, Vick offered them coffee.

Isaac opened his notepad. He'd start with the soft approach in the hopes they would settle in. "Mrs. Coburn, you said you and Crystal were college roommates?"

Marta clasped her hands together in her lap. "Yes, that's correct."

"So you've known Crystal for a good while."
She nodded.

"Did Crystal talk to you about any troubles she'd been having? Was anyone bothering her?"

She shifted in her seat. "No. She seemed fine." *Well 'fine' wasn't exactly the right word.* Crystal had been happy. Extremely happy. But she wasn't going to say that.

"When did you last see her?"

"A few days before. We talked about redecorating her home."

Isaac remembered the samples on the table. The date stamp on the package indicated it had been delivered to the Coburn's on February 13, the day before Crystal was found dead. "A few days before?" Isaac asked.

"Oh, I don't remember exactly," she retracted. "We see each other…" she paused. "Or I should say, we *saw* each other quite often."

"And where were you on the morning of Valentine's Day?" Isaac asked.

"That's a funny question, detective," Blake interjected.

"I'm just wondering if she was in the area and saw anything suspicious, Mr. Coburn."

Blake nodded giving Marta the go ahead to answer.

"I was at home with our son, Matthew, who was sick that day."

"Did you see anything suspicious in the neighborhood that morning, Mrs. Coburn? Any strangers walking through? Any cars you didn't recognize?"

She looked down into her lap. "No, no strangers, no cars."

"So you were on good terms before she died?"

Before she died? "Yes," she confirmed. Because it wasn't until the day she died that Marta had started to hate her.

"So, the two of you didn't have any troubles?"

Blake leaned forward in his chair. "Where are you going with this, detective? I think we've established Marta and Crystal were good friends. Isn't that why we're here to help?"

"Even good friends can argue, Mr. Coburn," Isaac said. Actually, the closer the relationship the more volatile the disagreements could be. If Marta discovered her husband was having an affair with Crystal that certainly could be a motive for murder.

"Marta and Crystal had nothing to argue about, detective," Blake said.

"I'd like to hear that from Mrs. Coburn," Isaac said. He looked over at Marta who shifted in her seat.

"No, nothing to argue about," she said. "We were redecorating her home." She added as if it were proof positive everything was fine between them.

"Any particular reason she was redecorating?"

Marta shrugged. "Crystal was always looking for new things. She got bored easily and needed some excitement, I guess."

Blake could have answered that question, but chose to let it pass. It really was irrelevant at this point.

The accounts of others did not suggest Crystal was bored. In fact, quite the contrary. "We have heard from a few others Crystal may have had a new beau. Did she share anything about that with you?" Isaac watched Blake closely for his reaction to the question.

"No," she answered honestly. "And I'm certain she'd tell me if she did." *Unless it was my own husband,* she didn't add.

"She was in the midst of a divorce, detective," Blake interjected. "I can assure you, she did not have a new beau."

Isaac took this opportunity to turn his attention to Blake. "Mr. Coburn, where were you that morning?"

"At a CLE," he said. "C-L-E stands for Continuing Legal Education. They are seminars attorneys are required to take to keep their license."

Isaac was familiar with CLEs. His wife had been to many over the years. He also knew there would be a sign-in sheet and materials handed out at the start, but that didn't mean all attorneys actually stayed for the entire class.

Isaac continued without comment. "Did you recently purchase a ring, Mr. Coburn?"

Marta looked at her husband trying to keep the panic from her face. *How did they find that out?*

Blake nodded, now understanding the line of questioning. They found the Valentine's Day gift and he was now a suspect. "Yes, indeed I did," he said.

Marta felt her stomach tighten.
Blake reached over and touched Marta's hand. "It was a gift for my wife."

Isaac looked into Blake's face and searched for that twitch that would give away a lie.

"Surely you realized it was mine when you read the card." He looked at Isaac. "I'm sorry, I was so shocked by Crystal's death the last time we spoke, I didn't think to mention it."

Isaac searched his memory of the scene and then looked at his notes. "Card?" he asked. "We didn't see a card."

Blake furrowed his brow. "Really? Then how did you know it was mine?"

"A neighbor reported seeing you and Crystal purchasing it," Isaac reported.

Marta shifted in her seat.

"Oh? I don't remember seeing anyone from the neighborhood," Blake said. "Crystal helped me pick it out and kept it for me to pick up on Valentine's Day," he explained. "I'd like to have it back as soon as possible." He smiled regretfully at Marta. "Sorry, honey, it was supposed to be a surprise."

Marta smiled back, and kept quiet for fear her voice would betray her feelings. She grasped Blake's hand affectionately. *Isn't that the way loving couples behave toward each other?*

Plausible answer, Isaac concluded. But one more thing needed explanation. "Crystal's telephone records show that you and she had been in contact almost daily over the last several months."

"Yes, that's true." He looked sheepishly at Marta.

Isaac continued, "In fact, the last call she made was to you on the morning of her death."

"Oh?" he said. "I didn't get that call. I forgot my phone at home that morning." He looked to Marta for confirmation. "Isn't that right, honey?"

Marta nodded. Indeed he had. Right there on the entryway table.

On purpose? Isaac wondered. "Records show that you and Crystal were scheduled on a flight to Los Angeles this Friday, is that correct?"

"Yes, that is correct. But I can explain that."

Marta searched his face. *How? How in the world would he explain that?*

They heard a knock at the door. An officer leaned in and gave Isaac a thumbs-up and then closed the door behind him.

Isaac regarded Blake. While they were unable to get any prints off the skillet, the barrel of the gun had two fingerprints that didn't belong to Crystal or Garrett. Forensics had just given him confirmation they belonged to Blake Coburn. "Do you own Steger boots, Mr. Coburn?"

Blake looked quizzically at Isaac. "Boots?"

Yes, he does, thought Marta. But Marta knew it hadn't been Blake wearing them that morning. It had been her. The excruciating memory of that day was forever etched in her brain.

◆ ◆ ◆

Matt had finally fallen back to sleep after a tough night being ravaged by the flu. Marta needed a nap herself, but had promised Crystal she'd deliver the decorating samples. She looked at the clock. If she hurried, she could drop off the samples and get back home before Crystal and Garrett returned from their counseling session. Sleeping Matt wouldn't miss her, and she wasn't in the mood for small talk with Crystal today. It seemed like the perfect solution. She pulled her jacket on over her pajamas, slid her slippered feet into Blake's boots and grabbed her mittens. She gathered the paint and countertop samples and stepped outside. A layer of ice covered the stairway, so she grasped the railing, stepped down cautiously, and then headed down the sidewalk through the snow. The cold wind blew her hair and she wished she had thought to wear a hat. She arrived at Crystal's and took the key from between the bricks on the right side of the door and let herself in.

She pulled off the boots and started up the stairs. She smelled the morning coffee and saw the light still on in the kitchen. She shook her head with disapproval. Crystal never had listened to her warnings about the importance of conserving energy. She clicked off the light and went into the dining room to leave the samples on the table. As she placed the package on the table, she spied a jewelry box with a Valentine's Day banner across the top. She rolled her eyes. *Oh no*, she thought. This had to be Garrett's desperate attempt to get Crystal back. Jewelry, it seemed, was always the way to Crystal's heart. How she hoped it wouldn't work this time. Curious, she opened it and saw a beautiful sterling ring with a round ruby stone surrounded by diamonds. As expected, it was gorgeous. The casino jeweler had impeccable taste. She pulled it out and slipped it on her finger. Not as extravagant as past gifts, but since Garrett no longer had full access to Crystal's money, it was probably nicer than he could afford. She started to remove the ring from her finger and noticed a card. *A card?* she thought with surprise. *That was new.* It was easy to have the casino jeweler choose a ring for him, but did Garrett actually take the time to pick out a card? He truly must be getting desperate. Perhaps this was how he made up for the size of the ruby. He must have seen how happy Crystal had been lately. *The kind of happy that comes from getting a dead weight like him off your back.* Marta adamantly hoped Crystal would remain firm in her decision. She needed to remember to call and encourage Crystal to stick to her guns. It was obviously the best thing for her.

Marta sat down. She picked up the envelope and inspected it. Unsealed. She flipped it back and forth in her fingers. Then, unable to stop herself, she took a peek. The front of the card showed a picture of a loving couple, nestled together on a rock overlooking the water. She practically laughed out loud at how absurdly dissimilar this was to the boxing match they called their marriage, leaving her to believe Garrett had the jeweler choose the card as well as the ring.

She opened it, and inside in fancy script it said, *"Especially today, I hope you feel how much I love you and how grateful I am to have you in my life. You take my breath away."* It was signed in that familiar hand, *"To the woman who makes my dreams come true. All my love, Blake."* She blinked. *"All my love, Blake,"* she read again. "All my love, Blake," she whispered as the tears welled up and streamed down her face. She stared at the card unable to believe her own eyes. It couldn't be. Not Blake, too. Crystal was supposed to be her friend. *How could she?* Marta crumpled the card and shoved it in her pocket, then stumbled down the hallway to the bathroom for a tissue.

She wiped her face and stared at herself in the mirror. She grasped the vanity with both hands. "You knew it was bound to happen," she said to the image in the mirror. *Inevitable*, she thought resignedly. She blew her nose and wiped her face. "I hate you, Crystal," she said out loud. "I hate you Crystal!" she screamed, as she started back down the hallway. And that's when she saw her.

Chapter 22

Captain Petruco paced back and forth in front of his mahogany desk waiting for the test results. "I did good today, Pop," he said to the man in the photo on the wall. "The press was all over me, but I put in a good performance. You would have been proud."

Sergeant Petruco had been an exemplary cop. From all reports, he was on his way to the top. But tragically, he was killed in the line of duty leaving behind his wife and teenage son. A son who vowed to continue his father's legacy.

"He got away from us, though," the younger Petruco continued, referring to Garrett Holt who was still on the lam. "Sneaky bastard." He stood in front of the photo and crossed his arms over his chest. "He could be anywhere by now." He shook his head. "I'm surrounded by incompetence. One lets him go, then the other one loses him."

He heard a knock at the door. "Come in," Petruco said.

The officer opened the door and stepped inside, papers in hand.

"So?" Petruco asked.

"It's hers." The officer smiled.

While they didn't find much else, the search of Garrett's townhome had produced several bloody, long, blond hairs stuck to the carpet. Best guess is they had become stuck to the bottom of the killer's shoes. What happened to the rest of the clothing was still a mystery. It didn't look like the killer had showered or washed up in the townhouse as they didn't find blood residue in any of the sinks, drains or the shower. There were no bloody fingerprints either. But from the forensics results at the crime scene, it appeared the killer had worn gloves, and the gloves were most likely with the rest of the clothing. Interestingly, they also found a safety deposit box key that had been taped to the back of one of the bureau drawers. They were diligently trying to identify the location of the box, and now that the strands of hair matched the victim, they would easily get a search warrant for that as well.

Petruco slapped the desk. "We've got our man. Put out an all-points bulletin," he instructed. He ran his hands through the slick hair on his head. "I'll get the arrest warrant." He focused his bird eyes on the officer. "I want every available man, woman and dog out there searching the city for him," he commanded. "Get his picture to the news media ASAP."

"Yes, sir!" The officer hurried out the door to get the word out.

Petruco straightened his collar and looked at the photo. "I'd better get spiffed up, Pop. It's show time." He'd first stop at the judge's office to get the warrant. Then he would assemble the press. They would come with microphones extended and cameras rolling, and hang on his every word. In no time, Garrett's face would appear on news reports everywhere. The whole country would be on alert for Garrett Holt.

♦ ♦ ♦

Red stepped up to the counter. The barista with the rainbow painted nails stared at him. "Remember me?" he asked.

She looked at him. "Should I?"

He sighed. He'd scoured every nook and cranny up and down the alley behind the coffee shop looking for clues as to where Garrett Holt had gone, hoping he'd find something the team missed yesterday, but to no avail. He was cold, disgraced and worried he'd be out of a job if he didn't find Holt soon. Garrett's townhouse search hadn't offered up much help. It was almost like he didn't really live there. They would keep tabs on his bank and credit card activity to see if they could get a lead on his whereabouts, but so far there hadn't been any transactions since before Red last saw him here, in this very coffee shop. He doubted this gal would shed any light either. "I was here yesterday."

A blank stare. "Oh."

"Behind a big guy with short cropped blond hair."

"Oh yeah. I hear the cops were looking for him yesterday." She sized him up. "You a cop?"

"I am."

"Good 'cause they got it all wrong."

"They do?"

"Yeah, they called him 'Garrett'. But his name is Bob. Lydia didn't know 'cause he doesn't come in on her shift, but I straightened her out."

"Does he come in often?" Red asked.

"Every month or so. I remember him because he always pays with cash and never leaves a tip."

Red pulled a five out of his wallet and shoved it in the jar.

She smiled. "Appreciated." She pointed to the back booth. "Always sits in the back booth after the dude in the suit goes."

"The dude in the suit?"

"Yeah, *that's* 'Garrett.' See? They got it wrong. He pays with cash too." She stuck out her tongue. "I hate that," she said. "Funny how they always show up on the same day. Like a routine or something."

"The dude in the suit's name is Garrett?" For some reason he wanted to jump over the counter and kiss her right then.

"Yeah," she said. "Always looks nervous."

"Do they know each other?"

She shrugged. "They never talk, but it's the same thing every time. Garrett comes in and has his coffee, then leaves as soon as Bob gets his coffee." She scrunched up her nose. "I always thought it was weird. Does it have something to do with why you're looking for Bob?"

"I think Bob's been messing with you," Red said. "He really *is* Garrett. Not sure who the other dude is, but I'd sure like to ask him some questions."

She looked confused.

"Mind if I check out the booth?" Red asked.

"Knock yourself out," she said.

Red scoured the booth, finding nothing but old gum stuck underneath. While he hadn't tracked down Garrett, at least he had something new to report. He got into his car and dialed the station. Peg picked up.

"Hey Peg," he said feeling like the leper of the department.

"Hey Red. How you doing?" she asked sympathetically. "Vick told me what happened."

Of course he did. "Ah, yeah. Well I have some new information," he said.

"I knew you would."

"Is Isaac around?" he asked.

"He's still interviewing the Coburns. Should I have him call you when he's through?"

"Nah, I'm on my way in. Tell him I'll be scouring the security footage from the coffee shop and to stop by my office when he's through."

Chapter 23

Isaac watched his face. "Yes, Mr. Coburn, Steger boots."

"I do," he said. "But what does that have to do with Crystal's murder?"

All Isaac saw was complete confusion on Blake's face. "Mrs. Rupp saw a pair of Steger boots in the entryway that morning," he said.

"A lot of people have Steger boots, Detective."

"She also said she didn't notice any unusual vehicles or people in the area that morning." He looked to Marta. "Which Mrs. Coburn corroborates. Isn't that right?"

Marta wrung her hands. *Had she said something wrong? Something incriminating?* "That's right," Marta confirmed. "But Blake left very early that morning."

Blake glanced at Marta. He scratched his brow. "As I said, I was at a CLE that morning. Please contact the

Minnesota CLE Conference Center in Minneapolis, and they will confirm my attendance."

"The last telephone call Crystal made was to your number, Mr. Coburn. May we see your phone?"

His phone? Marta thought with alarm. *They wanted to see his phone?* All along she thought they'd suspect Garrett, but this man was practically accusing Blake of the crime.

Blake pulled out his cell phone. "I told you, I forgot my cell phone at home that morning, so I did not receive her call. But it is not surprising she would call me," he said. "I was her attorney."

Marta shifted in her seat. *Her attorney? Since when?*

"Did she leave you a message?" Isaac asked.

"No. I didn't see any message," Blake said.

"May I look?"

"Certainly."

"Open it, please," Isaac requested.

Blake placed his thumb on the button and unlocked the phone. He touched the telephone icon, looked at his messages, and handed the phone to Isaac. "I don't see any message from Crystal on the fourteenth."

Marta's eyes shifted back and forth between the men. She felt her inner temperature rise. If the questioning continued on like this, she would have to tell them she was the one who had deleted that message and she really didn't want to do that.

Isaac looked and didn't see any message, and even more importantly, didn't see a record of the call either. While earlier calls and later calls abounded, Crystal's final call was not there. He looked at Blake. Something wasn't right here. "You were her attorney, Mr. Coburn?"

"Yes, that's right."

"Was this in connection with the divorce?"

"No, I'm an employment lawyer. This was in connection with a job."

Marta stifled a laugh. *Crystal? A job? He's lying*, she thought to herself. Crystal would never want to work.

Blake held up his pointer finger to request a moment, turned toward Marta and took her hands in his. "Marta, I wanted to share this with you under different circumstances," he began. "Crystal wanted to tell you right away and it wasn't easy to keep her from doing so." Blake smiled and raised his eyebrows. "You know how she could be when she wanted her own way." He looked toward Isaac. "The detective is right. We had been spending a lot of time together and I couldn't tell you about it."

Marta stared at him in disbelief. *Where was he going with this?*

"Crystal was looking at a job?" Isaac asked.

"Yes, a headhunter had contacted her and I was handling the negotiations."

Marta creased her forehead. *Negotiations?*

"With the number of calls you two shared it must have been quite an important position," Isaac remarked.

"Yes, it was. Crystal was going to be the new spokesperson for a new jewelry line on the Home Shopping Network."

"What?" Marta blurted out.

"You were not aware of this Mrs. Coburn?" Isaac asked.

It was preposterous. "No, I wasn't," she replied to Isaac, trying to sound calm. Marta searched Blake's face. She didn't believe it for a second. If Crystal had been offered a position on television, she would have shouted it to the world.

Blake touched Marta's shoulder apologetically. "One of the company executives was interviewing artists to paint a family portrait." He looked at Isaac. "Marta mentioned you visited the house with Edna. Did you notice the painting of Crystal in the family room?" Then, without waiting for an answer, he said. "Of course you did, how could you miss it?"

Marta stifled a groan.

Isaac and Vick exchanged a look. They remembered. The portrait Vick wanted to take home.

"The artist that painted the portrait was one of those interviewed," Blake informed them. "When the executive saw the painting of Crystal in the artist's portfolio, he decided she would be the perfect spokesperson for his jewelry line."

"Good choice," the previously quiet Vick approved.

Blake looked at Vick, disheartened. In these last few months he had been dismayed to confirm that most men looked at Crystal as a decoration or a toy. However, he also saw that Crystal had learned to use their chauvinism in her favor. He smiled to himself. They underestimated her at every turn. "We had been in negotiations for months. They wanted to be sure all negotiations were completely private so they interviewed Crystal by Skype several times and all of our meetings took place away from my office. Supposedly these networks spy on each other. Crystal and I found it easiest to meet during my son's hockey games."

Where they would *innocently* hug and cheer with each goal, Marta realized. *How had she ever thought otherwise?*

"We had flights to go to Los Angeles this weekend to sign the final paperwork." Blake took Marta's hand. "I'm so sorry we couldn't tell you about it, but we were required to sign an iron clad nondisclosure agreement." He looked at Isaac and Vick. "I had a conference with the company the morning after Crystal's death to let them know of her passing. They instructed me not to reveal anything about the contract unless absolutely necessary. Honestly, I never thought I'd have to divulge this to cover myself." He turned to Marta. "Not being able to tell you was the hardest thing in the world for Crystal."

Marta's eyes started to tear. It all made sense now. That was what Crystal was so happy about. Not a new beau. Not an affair with Blake. But because the world would finally have the opportunity to worship her. It was indeed the perfect role for Crystal. And now she was dead. There was no bringing her back. What had she heard Crystal say in her voice message that morning? 'Blake honey, don't try to stop me. I know we've discussed this, but I just can't keep it secret any longer. I'm going to tell Marta later today.' How she wished she would have known this was what Crystal intended to tell her.

Isaac took a breath. He would certainly check into Blake's attendance at the CLE and Crystal's job opportunity. He was immediately inclined to believe Blake's story, but then where were the card and the ring that were supposed to be a gift for his wife? And who was wearing those boots? His gaze landed on Marta, who looked like she had just run a marathon.

Chapter 24

ather John strapped on his snow shoes, grabbed his poles and headed toward the river bank. "C'mon Scout!" he called to his shepherd. Scout bounded past with enthusiasm.

Father John reveled in another clear, crisp, Minnesota morning and the replenishing peace and quiet a hike along the Minnesota River bank provided. Despite the frequent drifting of snow that accumulated as the wind twisted and turned down the river and through the trees, the snowshoes kept him on top, while Scout leapt through the mounds that were sometimes up to his collar.

Scout sprinted off ahead. "Scout!" Father John called. Scout obediently bounded back, ran a circle around Father John to be sure he was okay, then took off again. Father John shook his head. "Silly pup."

This was their Friday morning ritual, and Scout's favorite event of the week. He loved having the freedom to run with abandon, but, like clockwork, always circled back to check on his master. So when Scout didn't reappear after several calls, Father John became concerned. He hustled along the dog's tracks as they led closer to the riverbank. "Scout!" he called out, his anxiety increasing. The ice on the river should be firm, but the flow underneath could reveal soft spots, and if one fell through, they could be carried along under the ice. Father John finally spotted him a little farther down under the Highway 41 bridge and a wave of relief ran through him. "Scout!"

Scout lifted his head and looked at him, tail wagging wildly. He then grabbed something from the ground and scampered back along his own path. With exuberant excitement, Scout handed over his new found treasure. To Father John's horror, it was a bloodied sweatshirt. Father John immediately recognized the significance of this find. He had heard the news reports. He quickly plucked the leash from his pocket and hooked it onto Scout. *Could they have just found the missing man?* He pulled out his cell phone and dialed 911.

The police arrived shortly and hustled down the riverbank. There was no dead body. But Scout had found the best lead they had so far—a white kitchen garbage bag filled with bloodied clothing.

Isaac got the call at home and hightailed it to the station.

"Looks like he dropped the bag off the bridge," Vick told him. The bridge stood halfway between Crystal Holt's home and her estranged husband, Garrett's townhouse. "Garrett must have chucked it on his way home."

"Pretty smart to use white, it blended right in with the snow," Red said.

"Indeed," Isaac agreed. And to hide it further, the contrasting colored pull strings used to close and seal the bag had been removed, so no other color could give it away. The bag had to have been left by someone with at least enough foresight to consider this detail.

"It seems he's smarter than we thought," Vick said.

In contrast to Vick's conclusion, Isaac felt this was just another reason to discount Garrett Holt as the killer. But, he had to admit, all the facts pointed in Holt's direction. "Red, I saw your report on the coffee shop visits," Isaac said, and despite Red's earlier condemnation of Isaac which Isaac had not forgotten, he added, "Good sleuthing."

Vick placed his fists on his hips looking like Superman without the cape and scrutinized Isaac. "As unnecessary as that sleuthing should be." He shook his head. "I don't know what's up with you on this one. Seems like your ESP is on the glitch. You should have never let that murderer get away. He should already be behind bars," he declared. Vick then turned his attention to Red. "Or at the very least, still under surveillance."

Isaac ignored him. "Sounds like Garrett and the man in the suit were making exchanges of some kind," he said to Red. But, exchanges of what? Information? Numbers? Instructions? Money?

"Agreed," Red responded, grateful for the opportunity to avoid confrontation with Vick. "Maybe Garrett was paying off the suit to kill his wife." He used his fingers to make quotation marks in the air around the words 'the suit.'

Isaac had already considered and rejected this scenario. "Maybe."

"Disagree," Vick interjected. "Jaguar Garrett did it. Nobody would leave that car behind unless they were guilty of murder."

"Disagree," Red countered. "He'd leave it behind if he were guilty of hiring a hit man."

Vick shook his head. "We found bloody hair in Garrett's townhouse. Clearly, he did it."

Isaac put a hand on each of their shoulders to stop the bickering. "Can we all agree that it seems highly unlikely the man in the suit's name was also Garrett?" he began.

They both nodded.

"So the question is, why would the one in the suit use Garrett's name?" he asked them.

"Good question," Vick said. He turned toward Red. "If 'the suit' was a hit man, why would he use Garrett's name?"

Red ran his hand through his curly red locks. He knew that his fragile alliance with Vick wouldn't last long and Vick's current attitude confirmed Red was back on Vick's unpopular list. "Maybe it was some kind of insurance in case he got caught, so that he could drag Garrett down with him," Red suggested.

"You reported the barista said the one who called himself Garrett looked nervous," Isaac continued.

"Yep. That's what she said," Red confirmed.

Given Red's earlier report of what happened at the casino and now this, it sounded more like blackmail to Isaac than anything else. But blackmail for what? "Sounds to me like the real Garrett was leaning on him," Isaac said. "'The suit' probably used Garrett's name so if anything ever happened to him, we could tie Garrett to it."

Vick flicked his pointer finger at Isaac giving his approval. "Now that makes sense," he said. "He's already killed his wife, he might have loose ends to tie up. If I were 'the suit,' I'd be very nervous."

"I saw them on the security footage from yesterday," Red told them. "And am looking for more visits to see if I can find a pattern or some kind of exchange." In fact, he was desperately searching, trying to redeem himself. "I'll let you know as soon as I find something."

Isaac nodded, thankful they now had a new direction. Blake Coburn's story had checked out and he even had a plausible explanation as to how his fingerprints ended up on the gun. There had been no affair, just neighborhood gossip concocted from misinterpreted appearances.

The door opened and a forensics team member walked in still in her plastic lab coat and hair net carrying the white garbage bag and its contents in a plastic bin. "Get your gloves on, men. Here it is."

Isaac, Red and Vick did as they were told.

"Hi, Sheila," Vick said with a wink. He snapped the plastic glove around his wrist.

Sheila smiled coyly. "Hi, Vick."

Red rolled his eyes.

"These are definitely the clothes Crystal Holt's killer was wearing when she was shot," she said. "We have blood splatter and skin tissue galore." She held up a sweatshirt for their viewing.

Isaac furrowed his brow. "What size is it, Sheila?"

Sheila looked at the tag in the neckline. "Medium."

Isaac peered into the plastic bin. "And the pants, what size are they?"

She set down the sweatshirt and pulled up the sweatpants. "Also a medium."

Isaac looked back and forth between Red and Vick. They were all thinking the same thing. "There's no way Garrett Holt would fit in those clothes," he said. He turned toward Sheila. "Did you find any hair fibers?"

"Yes," she confirmed. "Several long blond hairs belonging to the victim, and a few shorter dark hairs. We're pretty sure they don't belong to the dog, but are checking that out as we speak."

"Any shoes?" Red asked.

Sheila shook her head.

"Gloves?" Vick asked.

"No, but this was also in the bag," she announced. She held up an Apple watch. "We should be able to get some

DNA from it and hopefully the IT geeks can figure out the password and get in."

Isaac grinned. "Now that's helpful."

Red grinned too. Since it now appeared Garrett couldn't be the killer, maybe it wasn't such a big deal that Red had lost him. In fact, maybe it was even somewhat fortuitous since it was only because of Red's losing him that he found out about 'the suit.' He looked at Vick and gave him a look that said 'take that'. *'The suit' would fit in those clothes*, Red thought triumphantly.

The wheels inside Isaac's head began to turn in new directions, opening up the field of possible perpetrators. "Sheila, can you tell if these are men's or women's sizes?" he asked.

Red narrowed his eyes at Isaac. "They look like men's clothes to me."

"Can't tell," Sheila said. "Pretty generic label."

Vick brushed an imaginary piece of lint off his shirt calling attention to his well-toned chest. Sheila swooned right in front of their eyes. "Kind of on the small side," he said.

Peg stuck her head in the door just in time to hear Vick's comment. She blushed. Red noticed. "More good news, men," she said. "They found Garrett's safety deposit box."

"Do we have a search warrant?" Isaac asked.

Peg held it up in her hand. "Right here."

Isaac looked at his dysfunctional team. "Let's go, boys."

They pulled into the Wells Fargo parking lot fifteen minutes later. The loan officer led them to the vault, let them in, and found Garrett's safety deposit box. He turned the key, pulled the box and took them to a small, private room to view the contents.

Isaac opened the lid. He saw a single manila envelope. He picked it up with gloved hands and dumped the contents on the table. A couple of flash drives and some printed photos fell out. Isaac picked up the photos to examine them. They were intimate photos of a man and woman in an outdoor setting, possibly a park or arboretum. The first one showed them kissing under a tree, but the woman's hair fell in a way that made it hard to make out their faces. The next was taken from behind as they walked along a path with arms around each other's waists. In the next, the couple was still walking the same path, but the man had turned toward the camera as if he had responded to someone calling his name. His face was clear.

"I know that guy!" Isaac and Red shouted simultaneously. They looked at each other, surprised.

"You do?" they again asked simultaneously.

Red nodded and smiled. "That's 'the suit.'"

Isaac nodded and grinned. "And I know who he is. Let's get the Apple watch," Isaac said. "We have a visit to make."

◆ ◆ ◆

Fifteen minutes later they were on their way to Willow Lane. The early evening sun had begun its descent casting pinks and oranges on the white snow cover. The icy branches on the trees glistened and the cardinals chirped happily.

Isaac and Vick headed up the walkway, while Red sat ready, car running, in case their target tried to flee. Two more squad cars had pulled over at the end of the block, also ready to take chase. Isaac glanced at the picture window curtain to see if anyone was watching. He was relieved to see no movement inside. It would be best if their arrival was unexpected. Isaac stood to the left and rang the doorbell, and Vick stood directly in front of the door, body camera rolling.

Patty swung the door open, and she looked back and forth between them. She scowled at Vick, and then focused on Isaac. "Hello detective. I suppose you're here to thank me for my assistance in finding Crystal's killer." She had heard that a warrant was out for Garrett's arrest. *And it was about time,* she thought. Everyone knew it was him. "I told you you should have arrested him. I knew he'd run."

"I'm returning something to you," Isaac said, and held out the plastic bag for her to view.

"Howard's Apple watch!" she exclaimed.

"Are you sure this is Howard's?" Isaac asked, as Vick filmed.

"Oh yes," she confirmed, then shot a look at Vick as if he had stolen it when he was there last. "He received the Apple watch for managing the telecom merger." She smiled proudly. "Series four," she added to make sure they were suitably impressed. "That's how much they think of him. No one else could have handled it. That's why he's in such high demand."

"Is Howard here?" Isaac asked. "We'd like to return it to him."

She turned toward the stairway "Howard!" she called, "there's someone here to see you." She snarled at Vick certain he had been caught red-handed and was here to answer for his crime. "He's upstairs packing. Off on another business trip. They just can't do without him," she said. "Well, stomp off that snow and step inside. You're letting all the cold air in."

They did as they were told and she closed the door behind them.

"Howard!" She called up the stairs again.

Howard came around the corner at the top of the stairs looking more like a hen-pecked husband than a hitman. "What is it?" he mumbled, then stopped dead in his tracks and stared wide-eyed at the officers.

"Howard, they have your Apple watch! I didn't even know it was missing." She shot another look at Vick. "But someone must have had sticky fingers."

Howard had wondered what happened to that watch. With all the turmoil that day, he hadn't noticed it was missing until he was safely inside the hotel room. At that point, there was no going back to retrace his steps. Now it could be his undoing. Seeing no other option, Howard reluctantly descended the stairs. "Oh, hello officers."

"Look, Howard." Patty pointed at the plastic bag.

"That's not my watch," he declared as he stared into the plastic bag and beads of sweat appeared on his forehead.

"Well, of course that's your watch," Patty said. "See the company logo on the band? It's the one you got for managing the telecom merger." She looked at Isaac. "He really is a master with these acquisitions. The company would be lost without him."

"That's not my watch, Patty," Howard repeated, and gave his wife a look that clearly was intended to shut her up.

"I believe we have some of your clothing at the station as well," Isaac said. "We'd like you to come identify it."

Patty's jaw dropped. "Clothing?" She looked to her husband. "Howard?"

"Why don't you come with us now," Isaac said.

All the air left Howard and he looked like he was about to faint. His watch must have fallen off when he stripped down and shoved the clothes in the bag. He knew now all chances of denial were gone.

"Howard?" Patty repeated.

"Yes," he said resignedly to the officers. "Yes, that would be fine." He looked at his wife. "You stay here, I'll be just a minute." He stepped outside into the frigid air without getting his coat. Vick took his arm and they led him to the squad car waiting in the driveway.

"Howard?" Patty called out. "What's going on Howard?"

Chapter 25

It was a quiet ride to the station as the weight of his circumstance settled in on Howard. In some ways, he would be relieved to be able to unburden himself. But he also realized that life, as he knew it, was over. Ending Crystal's life also ended his own.

Isaac and Vick sat across from Howard at the same table they had sat when interviewing Garrett only two days ago. Two days ago, when Isaac had let Garrett go free and Red had lost him. But all of that had been quickly forgotten now that the real killer had been found. Petruco and Red watched from behind the glass, eager for the confession to begin.

Howard sat stiffly in his seat. "It was an accident," he claimed. "She wasn't supposed to be home." His head fell to his chest. "She wasn't supposed to be home," he repeated. He looked up with desperate eyes. "I saw the car leave."

Isaac watched as Howard wrung his hands. "Let's start at the beginning," Isaac directed. "Why were you there?"

Howard let out a deep sigh. "Garrett was blackmailing me so I went there to look for the pictures so it would stop." He rubbed his temples. "It had to stop."

"The pictures?"

There was no use sugar-coating it. "I was having an affair," Howard admitted. "Garrett had photos of us."

They had all seen the photos. And as far as blackmail photos go, these were quite innocuous. One couldn't tell for sure who the parties were in the kissing photo. Otherwise, it could be two good friends walking arm in arm. No X-rated scenes. "Would it have been so bad if those photos had come out in the open?" Isaac asked, dumbfounded as to why that would be reason enough to take another's life.

A tear fell down Howard's cheek. *The pictures would certainly be out in the open now,* he thought to himself. *What had he done?* How he wished he could just rewind the tape and erase the events of that morning. The events of that morning that now haunted him every waking moment.

◆ ◆ ◆

Howard remembered clearly how he saw Garrett's car back out of the driveway and head down Willow Lane that morning. When it turned right at the corner, Howard put on his gloves, pulled up the hood of his sweatshirt, grabbed the duffle bag, crossed the street and headed up the walkway to the front door. In a crack in the brick above the door he found the key. Just where Patty said they kept it. He took a quick look up and down the street. He didn't see anyone. He turned the key and let himself in, then returned the key to its hiding place. He figured he'd have at least a couple of hours before they would return. He started in the room they called the "office," which contained nothing but a desk. On the desk sat a pink laptop, and a pink iPad. They most likely belonged to Crystal, but he wasn't going to leave anything behind. He shoved them into the duffle bag and looked through the drawers. Along with a bunch of pens, pencils, note pads and batteries, he found a bag of flash drives. "Yes," he said under his breath and added those to his stash.

He then moved on to the master bedroom and started with the bureau, opening drawers and digging through. He dumped the jewelry box on the dresser and sifted through looking for more flash drives.

What he didn't know, however, was that Crystal had not gone to the counseling session that day. She had just finished her bath, and was on the other side of the wall in the large room she used as her closet trying to decide what she would wear for the day. This momentous day when she planned to divulge her incredible secret to her best friend.

Her headphones slid off as she pulled down a blue sweater from the shelf, and she heard noises coming from the bedroom. *Crap,* she thought to herself. She was certain Garrett had returned to continue their fight. She chided herself for not thinking to take the key so he couldn't get back in after she kicked him out earlier. He'd been manic. Pleading with her one minute and angry with her the next. She should have known he would not give up easily.

She listened intently through the wall. *What was he up to anyway?* she wondered. *Why hadn't he called out to her? Why was he sneaking around out there?*

She crept around the corner into the bathroom that connected the closet and bedroom, to try to get a look at what he was doing. She could see in the reflection of the mirror over the vanity that her jewelry had been strewn across the dresser. Garrett had made it very clear earlier that he needed money. He had begged her for money. *Would he stoop to stealing from me?* She moved farther into the bathroom to get a better look just as a hooded figure passed by the doorway. She stopped dead in her tracks. A shock wave of alarm ran through her body. That was not Garrett. She stepped back into the closet and searched the pockets of her robe for her cell phone and then remembered she had left it on the bedside table. *What should I do?* She looked around the closet for places to hide. *But what if he comes in and finds me?* She would be trapped with nowhere to go. Panic set in. She had to protect herself. She had to get out of there.

She found the gun tucked under the comforter on the top shelf. She grasped the butt of the pistol with her right hand. Holding the firearm at her side, she crept around the corner into the bathroom that connected the closet and bedroom. She looked down at the weapon in her hand and took the safety off.

She mustered all the courage she had and stepped out from the bathroom. "Don't move," she shouted, holding the gun out in front with two hands looking like one of Charlie's Angels. "Put your hands up."

The hooded figure did as he was told.

She kept the gun trained on the intruder's back and moved toward the bedside table to retrieve her cell phone.

"Wait," the hooded figure said.

The voice was familiar. "Howard?" she exclaimed.

He turned toward her. "Yeah."

She dropped her arms to her sides. "Howard, what are you doing here?"

His head fell to his chest. "I'm looking for some pictures Garrett took."

"Pictures?" she asked. "Couldn't you just ask for them?"

Howard sighed deeply. He looked at her with pleading eyes. "Garrett's blackmailing me."

"Garrett? Blackmailing you? Whatever for?"

"He has pictures of me with a woman," he told her. "A woman who is not Patty."

She put her hands on her hips. "You were having an affair?"

He nodded sheepishly.

She pointed at him, gun still in hand. "*You* were having an affair?" she repeated.

"Yes," he said. "Please put the gun down."

Crystal couldn't believe her ears. The upstanding, honorable, virtuous Howard was having an affair. "Garrett didn't mention this."

"He's been extorting money from me for over a year now," he said. "He's relentless."

"A year now? That can't be right. I'd know if he were doing something like that."

"I think he has a gambling addiction."

Addiction? "Sure, he likes to bet on sports and play craps, but I wouldn't call it an addiction."

"He's in deep," Howard said.

She shook her head. "No, I don't believe it," she said. *But it would explain his demands for more money*, she thought to herself. She cocked her head at him. "How did he find out about your affair?"

"He saw us at the casino."

She waved the gun in his direction. "You and who?"

He took a step back. "It doesn't really matter, does it?"

She looked at him incredulously. "It doesn't matter?" she snapped. "I'll bet SHE thinks it matters."

He could feel the heat from her eyes. His face turned crimson. "It's no one you know," he answered evasively. "Crystal, please put the gun down," he implored. "Let's talk."

She started to pace.

"I just need to find the photos to stop the blackmail," he said. "Garrett has prints and the images could be on a laptop or flash drive. Will you help me find them? I'm desperate."

"Garrett doesn't live here anymore."

"He didn't leave anything behind?"

She stopped pacing and looked at him with resolve. "No. And I'll tell you how you stop the blackmail. You come clean to Patty."

"It's not that simple," he said.

"Of course, it's simple. Either you tell her, or I will."

"No, no you can't," he implored. "It's not just about me. It's, it's her sister."

"You're sleeping with her sister?"

"Yes, so please, please, please don't tell Patty," he pleaded. "Besides, I would think you, of all people, would understand."

She looked at him, confused. Patty certainly wasn't her favorite person and she believed it would be more than challenging to be married to her, but, "Why?" she asked.

"Well," he said. "You're sleeping with your best friend's husband."

Her eyes widened and then turned to fire. "I AM NOT!" she declared. "Where did you hear that?"

He took another step back. "P—Patty told me," he stammered.

"Patty told you?" she roared.

"She—she said everybody knows." But from Crystal's reaction, Howard sensed that Patty had it wrong.

"Everybody thinks I'm sleeping with Blake?" she exclaimed in horror as her arms flailed about. "Thanks to your gossiping wife?"

"No, no," he said to sooth her. "Crystal, put the gun down. We'll get this straightened out."

"Yes, we will. Right now. Let's go." She gestured with the gun toward the door.

Panic filled Howard's face. "Patty's not home."

She regarded him skeptically.

"She's at a fundraising event all morning. I promise, I'll make sure she knows you're not having an affair," he pledged, although he had no idea how he was going to do that without compromising himself. "And that she makes sure everyone else knows it too."

Her eyes narrowed. "And I'll make sure that she knows that YOU are," she vowed. *The perfect revenge for that rumor-starting busy body*, she thought with satisfaction.

Howard clasped his hands together, thrusting them in front of her face. "No, Crystal! I beg of you, please don't."

His sudden movement startled her. She grasped the pistol with both hands and aimed it at him. He had said it himself, he was desperate. "Don't come any closer," she warned.

"You can't tell Patty, it will kill her," he beseeched.

"Oh, I can and I will."

He couldn't let that happen. He lunged at her, grabbing the hands that held the gun. "Give me that," he demanded. "Just let me explain."

"Get away from me!" she shouted and pulled back on the gun.

In a flash, the gun fired. Crystal fell to the floor.

◆ ◆ ◆

"Howard?" Isaac called, summoning Howard back to the present. "Would it have been so bad if those photos had come out in the open?" he repeated.

Howard shifted uncomfortably in his seat. "It's my wife's sister. She's married, too. I wanted to protect her."

Isaac wasn't sure if he meant he wanted to protect his wife or her sister. "Enough to kill Crystal?"

"I never meant to hurt anyone," he said.

Maybe he hadn't set out to hurt anyone, but he certainly hadn't taken the time to avoid doing so either, Isaac thought to himself.

"It was an accident," Howard claimed again. "I just wanted it to stop. I just wanted to finally and completely remove the evidence once and for all so Garrett would stop threatening me."

It had been almost fourteen months since Garrett had spotted them on a romantic getaway to the Black Bear Casino, snapped those photos and demanded payment to keep his mouth shut. Howard had willingly paid after Garrett's assurance the pictures had not been sent elsewhere, and with the agreement that Howard, himself, would delete the photos from Garrett's cell phone. How could he have been so naïve? He never should have left that cell phone out of his sight. In hindsight, he should have made Garrett come with him when he made the withdrawal, but at that particular ◆ moment he didn't want them to be caught on the bank cameras together. Why he had believed for one instant that he could take Garrett at his word, was beyond comprehension. He should have known better. Garrett could not be trusted. Two weeks later, Garrett showed up at his door, printed photos in hand, and demanded more money. With Patty just feet away preparing their dinner, he was in no position to argue. So, the next day, certain Garrett would be back for more unless he did something about it, Howard called and tried to negotiate. But Garrett had the damning photos and the only concession Howard could finagle was to be allowed to make the delivery away from Willow Lane. And thus began the drop in the coffee shop.

"Garrett was threatening you," Isaac said.

Howard nodded. "Yes, he's in with some very bad people. He kept asking me for more money and more money." He dropped his forehead to the table and covered the back of his head with his hands. "I don't *have* any more money. It had to stop."

Isaac and Vick exchanged a look. They certainly remembered Garrett's rabid rant about money. They also remembered Red's report about the telephone calls at the casino. It all made sense now. Garrett owed big money and was squeezing it out of Howard. And now it was also obvious Garrett had pushed Howard too far—to the point of desperation. "So if Garrett was threatening you, why did you shoot Crystal?" Isaac asked.

He sat up straight. "I didn't shoot her," he proclaimed. "She had the gun pointed at me. I was just going to take it away and it went off." He moaned. "I didn't know it was loaded."

Isaac sat back in his chair. "Tell us what happened that day. From the beginning."

Howard took another deep breath. "I knew that Garrett and Crystal went to counseling every Thursday," he began.

"How did you know that?"

"My wife told me. She knows everything that happens in that household. She had an event to attend that morning, so it seemed like my opportunity to search the Holt's house undetected."

Howard gave an abbreviated and slanted version of that morning's events, white-washing his part to put himself in the best light possible. "She acted crazy," he declared. "I told her I just wanted to go, but she kept threatening to shoot. I had to get the gun away from her to save myself." Howard ran his hands through his hair. "She was about to give it to me, then she pulled it back and the gun went off." He looked pleadingly at Isaac and Vick. "You have to believe me, it was all a terrible accident." Howard covered his face with his hands and wept at the memory. "I didn't know what to do. I didn't know what to do," he repeated.

"So what *did* you do?" Isaac asked.

"I left as fast as I could." Tears covered his face.

Isaac handed him a tissue. "You left the house?" he asked.

Howard mopped his face and blew his nose. "Yes."

"Where did you go?"

"Home. To the garage. My bag was already packed, so I pulled out some fresh clothes and put the bloody clothes in a garbage bag."

"And then?"

"Then I got in my car and headed toward Garrett's." He looked at the table and shook his head. "I really needed to find those pictures."

That explained how the garbage bag ended up along the river, why Garrett's house was such a mess when Isaac first visited, and how Crystal's bloodied hair was found inside. But it didn't explain who hit Edna Rupp.

"You didn't go back to the Holt's house?" Isaac asked.

Howard looked at him, astonished at the question. "Oh, no."

After Howard's confession, the police descended on Patty's house to take the place apart, dust for prints, search in every drawer, spray luminol throughout, and touch all her paintings. She was despondent.

Chapter 26

Isaac helped Edna to the car. "I just can't believe it was Howard who shot Crystal. What a tragedy. And all because of men behaving badly." She shook her head and he thought he heard "tsk, tsk" come from her lips.

Isaac buckled his seat belt and backed down the driveway. They were unclear who had actually pulled the trigger, but it was certain that Crystal would still be alive if Howard hadn't been there. Isaac put the car into drive and headed down the street as the snow began falling. "Edna, Howard said he didn't hit you on the head."

She stayed unusually silent and watched the world speed past through the passenger side window.

"Edna?" he called over to her. "Howard said he didn't hit you on the head," he repeated in case she really didn't hear him the first time. "I don't think he'd admit to murdering Crystal but deny hitting you on the head."

"Look at them flakes," she exclaimed referring to the snow that had just started to fall. "The big puffy kind."

He glanced over at her. She was ignoring him. "That means someone else was there," he said.

"This is the best kind of snow," she declared. "Nice and easy to shovel."

"Edna, someone else had to be there," he said again.

"But not so good for snow balls."

"Edna, you're ignoring me."

She looked over at him and pat him on the leg. "Oh, I get to walking too fast, you know. I probably just slipped and fell."

"Edna, your hair was found on the back of the skillet."

"Huh. Imagine that. Big ol' skillet. Just too heavy for me, I guess. Must have knocked my own self out in the fall," she said. "Yep I'm sure of it. I'm just a silly old woman you know. Well, no matter." She focused her crisp blue eyes on him. "Don't go wasting good time on all that."

"Edna, do you know who hit you?"

"Whether I do or don't, don't make one wit of difference because I won't be filing any charges. I'm just a silly old woman who can't handle a skillet and that's all there is to it." And besides, after last night's visit, she knew there was a very good reason for the whack on her head. She would have done the same.

◆ ◆ ◆

It was just after 7:00 p.m. when Edna heard the doorbell.

Marta stood on the stoop, holding a large bouquet in her arms, with dread seeping through her veins. They had Howard in custody, and so it was time for her to come clean.

Edna opened the door. "Glory be! It's Marta! What beautiful flowers! For me?"

"Yes, dear. For you," Marta said. *And I won't blame you if you shove them in my face after what I've got to tell you*, she didn't add.

"Let me get these in some water," Edna said. "C'mon in, make yourself comfortable."

Marta hung her coat in the entryway closet and then took a seat in the living room. She wrung her hands nervously. "How are you feeling, Edna?" she called toward the kitchen.

"Better every day. And especially good now that you're here to visit."

"Aw, aren't you sweet!" *But you may not feel that way with what I have to share*, Marta thought to herself.

Edna came back in the living room carrying the vase and set it on the coffee table. "Daisies have always have been my favorites, you know." She smiled. "They're so cheerful and unassuming."

Marta did know. And it took visits to three floral shops to find them this time of year. She looked into Edna's blue eyes. "Edna, I have another confession to make."

"Are the flowers from Patty too?" Edna grinned mischievously.

Oh, if it were only that easy, Marta thought. "No, no. It's about Crystal— and you— it's really about you."

"Yes, dear?"

Marta took Edna's hand in hers. Edna needed to know. And while it wouldn't be the whole story, it would alleviate Marta's guilt. "I was there the day Crystal was killed."

"Oh?"

"I went to bring her samples for her redecorating. I let myself in and put the samples on the dining room table," she began.

"I saw those samples when I visited with the detective," Edna said. "Very nice choices, I thought." She smiled at Marta with approval.

Marta looked into her lap. Obviously, Edna didn't know where this was headed. "Well, it was cold that day," she continued.

"Oh, indeed it was. Terrible sleet early on, then the melting," Edna said.

"So, I needed a tissue," Marta told her. The cold air always made her nose run, so it was a plausible reason to get a tissue, she reasoned, and she didn't see any need to tell her the real reason she needed the tissue. "So, I went to the bathroom."

Edna nodded, dutifully following along.

"When I came back down the hall, I saw Crystal on the bedroom floor. I've never had a worse fright."

Edna gasped and put her hands to her face. "No!" she cried. "You saw her? Oh my dear! That would be a terrible fright!"

"Then I heard the garage door open. I know now it was you, but I thought it was the killer back to ransack the place or clean up the body or something. Edna, I freaked out. I ran into the kitchen to hide and grabbed the iron skillet from the stove." She took a deep breath and remembered how her whole body shook with fear. "I heard the footsteps come closer," she continued. "Your footsteps." How she wished she could take it all back. She remembered how, as the figure passed the doorway, she had swung the skillet and landed a blow on what she thought was the intruder's head. "Oh Edna, I'm so so so sorry, I didn't know it was you."

Edna looked at her compassionately. "Oh, my dear. How awful for you. Don't you worry yourself one little bit. I'm just fine," she assured her. "And you best believe I would have done the same thing," she added consolingly.

Marta reached over and hugged Edna while the tears streamed down her face. "I'm going to turn myself in," she said.

Edna sat back and held Marta by her shoulders. "You'll do no such thing. No harm done here. This'll be our little secret, you and I."

"Edna, I didn't mean to hurt you."

"I know you didn't, dear."

"I didn't know what to do," Marta said. She remembered watching in horror as Edna fell to the floor. "Oh Edna!" Marta had called out and dropped to her knees. Edna was out cold but, thankfully, still breathing. "Edna," she had called again. "Edna, wake up." She took her wrist and felt for a pulse. She needed to call 911, but realized she left her phone at home. "I need to get to my phone, Edna," she had said to her. "You just rest there. I'll get help." She had jumped up, bounded down the stairs, pulled on Blake's boots and ran out the door not bothering to close it behind her.

Marta then explained how, in a panic, she had struggled with the key in her door, then pushed through. How she ran through the house searching for her phone. How, just as she was going to head upstairs, she heard the sirens coming around the corner. How she ran to the door and watched with endless gratitude as the police arrived at Crystal's house. She looked at Edna. "I thanked God, Edna. I knew you must have come to and called them."

"Indeed, I did, dear. Thanks to that cold wind coming through the door you left open. You see? It all worked out just fine."

The tears started to flow again. "I thanked God they arrived to help you," Marta said. She remembered how she had stood in the doorway, with that same cold air washing over her, so glad they would help Edna and that Edna would be okay. But not Crystal. Crystal was not going to be okay.

"I'm glad you told me, dear. It's…" She paused and looked up as if the answer was hanging in the air. "What's that word the detective used yesterday?" she asked herself. "Oh yes— it's *cathartic*." She smiled. "And once we're done here, you can just forget it and move on."

Marta wiped her cheeks and nodded. "Edna, I don't know how to make this up to you."

"No need. Nothing but an accident, that's all there is to it," Edna declared. "You just keep this to yourself," she said. "I'm going to."

The rest of the tale, Marta knew, she would keep to herself. How she had stepped back into the house, closed the door and turned to find Blake's phone on the entryway table. How she took the phone and opened it, finding several messages, the latest one from Crystal. How she hit play and listened to Crystal say, "Blake honey, I've heard all your warnings." How she heard Crystal then go on and list Blake's warnings: "That it's not time. That you have more arrangements to make. That if anyone found out it would be the end of it all." How Crystal then said, "But I can't go on any longer like this. I'm going to tell Marta later today. Don't try to stop me. I know we've discussed this but I can't keep it secret any longer."

How Marta had sat statue-like and listened to it again. How her heart raced. How the words ran through her head: *Don't try to stop me? Would Blake? Could Blake?* How she had erased the message, placed the phone back on the table, and started to pace.

But no one needed to know that. No one needed to know she actually suspected her husband of the unthinkable— especially her husband.

✦ ✦ ✦

"Edna," Isaac said. "If you know, you need to report it."

"I'm telling you, detective," Edna said. "Don't go opening that can of worms, nothing good will come of it. Even if you think you have it figured out," which she suspected he did, "I won't press charges. Stop wasting the good tax payers' money on me. Let's let that sleeping dog lie."

Petruco would certainly agree with her, Isaac thought. He was making the most out of having caught the killer—and in three days, no less. So much so, that those pesky little details like whatever happened to Garrett Holt and who hit Edna Rupp were shoved under the rug. If brought back into the light, they would only take away from the commendations showered upon him. Isaac thought he had a pretty good idea of what had happened after Crystal's murder, and he viewed Edna's refusal to cooperate as confirmation that he was correct. That being the case, he was fine with leaving well enough alone. Edna was right. Nothing good could come from prosecuting the one who hit her with a skillet.

They pulled into the driveway. "Well here it is," he announced.

He came around the side of the car and opened the door for her. "Always a gentleman," she commended with a nod as she took his hand.

He took her arm and led her to the door.

Claudia set the new vase on the entryway table just as Isaac opened the door. Claudia smiled as the little sprite of a woman entered.

"Claudia, I'd like you to meet Edna Rupp, "Isaac said. "She has agreed to help us out with things around here."

"Welcome to our home, Edna. I'm looking forward to getting to know you." She reached out her hand and Edna grasped it with both of hers.

Edna's clear blue eyes smiled up at Claudia. "My dear," Edna said. "I don't think I've ever seen a more beautiful smile. You shine from the inside out, you do."

Claudia blushed.

Isaac winked at Claudia. "Told you you'd like her."

About the Author

Jennifer Anderson is a paralegal with a law firm in Minneapolis. She enjoys spending her free time with her husband at their island cabin in northern Minnesota.

9 781946 195531